Written and Illustrated by Candace Ball
Edited by Deb Hall
Cover Fonts by Peter Wiegel

To my family and my husband
Taylor for their continued
support.

Forever Eliza

Candace Ball

1

I make my way closer to the subway entrance, careful not to slip in any of the puddles on the sidewalk. I am glad the rain has let up the past few days, but the wind is still pretty chilly and the gray clouds block out the sun. No one seems to be bothered much by it, but everyone has an umbrella always at hand. I also carry a small umbrella in my purse, but my mind wanders and I forget about it even after the rain picks up. A few raindrops begin to bounce off my nose. I place the hood of my raincoat over my head and tuck in the sides of my long hair. I apply a thin layer of lip gloss, trying to distract myself and give myself another moment to think about what I'm about to do.

The crowds of people around me are getting thicker and tower over my small frame. Everything in this city seems to tower over me, but it is to my advantage. Maybe this is the reason I have been attracted to New York: to be overshadowed, remain invisible. No matter where I wander, I always end up back here. Having the appearance of a college-aged woman, I look like a lot of the people who live here. I could easily pass as an NYU student even though I am far from it. I am wearing my tight black skinny jeans, as they call them, which have holes in the knees, with my short black combat boots over my jeans. My thick jacket has deep pockets and a fur-lined hood. I sink my hands deeper into my pockets while struggling not to bump those passing me.

I told myself, one day I would accomplish something. I would do something that mattered. It feels unfair to work so hard at an amateur job in retail only to pay rent and stay hidden. A doubtful voice creeps up into my mind and tells me living a fulfilling life will be impossible. This option died a while ago with my old life. Even if I do manage to live in a way worth the time and effort, what will it all be for? By the time I start to get a little comfortable, I have to move on again. Any achievement I attain will mean nothing when I have to start over. I have places where I stay for a few years but never a home like the one I used to have. It seems useless to try anymore. I am always on the outskirts, always watching and never truly participating, leaving me with relationships that never delve beneath the surface.

I look up and see the entrance to the subway is only a few feet away. I descend the steps and plant my feet to avoid the wet areas. The different smells and the humidity waft over me as I glance through the moving throngs of people. Men and women make their way off the train, kicking up trash from the bottoms of their damp shoes. I take off my hood and smooth down my dampened, frizzy hair. I stand on the perimeter watching men and women make their way off the train, some on their way home from work and some about to start a late shift. There are businessmen in expensive-looking suits and women with designer purses and heels, others wearing casual secondhand outfits, and some muttering to themselves wearing ragged clothing. In the distance I can hear the violin of a street performer, one of many who come to work the subway. I jump back, letting a mouse scurry past me with its furry friend.

There must be some truth to what I was told a few days ago. What do I have to lose by coming here to see? Am I just being gullible, hoping this will give me some sense of fulfillment? Who in their right mind would follow the orders of a stranger? I am an idiot for believing this man. I berate myself until I notice a face standing out in the crowd. There is a man a few feet away who is standing very still, which looks unusual in contrast to the hustle of the subway. I take a few steps closer. He is looking out into the distance with a blank expression on his face. I walk toward him, putting myself only a few feet from him. His expression changes as his eyes meet mine.

An uneasiness forms in my chest as his absent expression turns into one more menacing, beckoning a challenge. His wicked smirk brings a heavy weight to my stomach. He is wearing a gray beanie down to his eyebrows, fingerless gloves, and a blue padded vest jacket. In a cautious manner, his gloved hands reach for his jacket and pull down the plastic zipper. My heart palpitates in my chest as anxiety threatens to take over. My thoughts all jumble together as I peer into the slight opening in his jacket. The adrenaline forces its way into my veins as he reveals the bomb strapped to his chest. I freeze. It's surprising no one around us notices. I want to wither up and scurry away like one of the subway rodents. What if I cannot complete the task assigned to me?

The past life I have tried so hard to push away comes to the very forefront of my mind. My long history can never be forgotten or escaped no matter where I live or whom I pretend to be. It will forever be ingrained in me despite my efforts to shove it down. In my attempts to bury it, I have only become more withdrawn and bitter over the last two centuries of my life.

In 1853 I was living on my estate in England with my six children and husband. I recall looking at my face in my vanity in the sitting room off my bedroom. As I did every morning, I brushed my hair with an ivory comb my husband had given me almost a year earlier on my birthday. I was almost thirty-five years of age. This was yet another reminder my body was not changing how it should be. Other women my age had at least a few gray hairs and wrinkles around the eyes. This never happened for me, and the longer time went on, the clearer I understood it would not. I looked more than a decade my junior. How much longer could I pretend, not only to myself but to others, that something was different?

Louise had helped me into my outfit this morning, like every other. Had she noticed something out of the ordinary? Louise was one of many who lived with us and helped us on our estate for the assurance of food and income. It would be hard to keep my secret safe with those who worked for us. I was not certain every person could be trusted to keep quiet.

This particular morning the children were to remain with the governess busy with their lessons until I got back from town. I needed to pick up a few items and also have some time away. We were halfway to town when the carriage began veering off the road. Something was not right. Within a moment, it was not possible to discern which direction was which. We were tumbling around in flashes of light and color, and it was all smearing together.

When I opened my eyes, I found myself back in my own bed, not certain how I had managed to get there or how much time had passed. I looked up at the face of my doctor, who wore a grim expression. I asked him what had happened without realizing the words were coming from my mouth. After some hesitation, first placing his items back into his bag, the doctor gave me the status of my health.

"It is very fortunate you are still with us," he began. "Besides your scrapes, you have suffered major injuries to your back. I am optimistic you may someday walk again, but never in the same manner as you had before."

Something inside me began to sink. There were bandages on my arms and legs. My legs were numb. How had this happened? All I could do was stay in bed and soak up the hopelessness surrounding me.

I woke up the next morning in a heavy fog. I looked to the empty chair on the side of my bed my husband must have pulled up earlier. He was probably in the other room. The sunlight poured into the room from a parting in the curtains. I pulled away my covers and rose to close them. How I longed for another hour of sleep. My hands paused on the curtains. I looked down, and when I saw the bandages, the events of the accident flooded to my memory. My legs were no longer numb.

I sat on the bed and began to pull off one of the bandages on my leg. The area where there must have been cuts before had fresh skin in its place. I pulled off the rest of the bandages one by one, each time surprised there were no signs of injury underneath. I balled up my bandages and threw them under my bed as tears came to my eyes. No longer could I continue to lie to myself by assuring myself I was normal. There was a day several years before my accident that had told me the truth of my condition, but I would not listen. It was not until after the accident I was forced to turn from my denial. The accident should have been fatal.

The years marched on, one after another. There was nothing I could manage to do besides pretend to become older in a way believable to those around me. Edmund encouraged me to press on after my many nights of contemplating what it could all mean or where it would lead. I had showed him my arms and legs after the accident. At first he could not believe it, but after a few years he understood. We continued to raise our family in our home and watched them leave one by one as they grew older. I wanted to hold on to time and make it slow down, but it slipped out of my grasp and left only a dull aching that always lingered in the background. In a few decades everyone I loved was gone.

It was after the turn of the century and all my children had passed. I decided to take a walk through the back walkways of my estate. I lifted up the sides of my mourning dress as I walked so it would not catch on the brush on either side of the dirt path. The mourning dress I wore was one of many I had owned and was already beginning to wear and fade. As I walked, I took little notice of the wildflowers growing along the path.

After a few minutes had passed, I looked up. There stood the grand marble mausoleum. Edmund commissioned it to be built on our property when he was alive. It stood tall and stark against the green landscape. The two marble women on top held their hands out, looking down at me with downcast expressions. The mausoleum held the bodies of my family members who were not buried with their own families.

Only a week before, there was a processional given to my youngest child, my son, who had passed away at the age of fifty-seven. I was only about two decades from reaching my hundredth birthday myself. No one knew. I felt like a ghost on my own property. I was known by everyone on my estate as a distant relative to the family. My husband and I had planned a farce processional for myself when I no longer wanted to pretend I was older with my makeup and wigs or imaginary "ailments." We had the staff replaced after my pretended death and then every few years after that to be sure no one suspected anything.

The iron bars were locked in place at the front of the mausoleum. My name was also engraved inside the beautiful but looming structure. My heart had remained there for a long time. The days I dreaded had finally come. I never wanted to think about what I would do when everyone I loved was suddenly gone. I had frequent nightmares where I would be calling out their names but no one would answer. It was only my own voice echoing off the walls. Nothing enabled me to be with them. Who would've ever thought death would be seen as a beautiful thing of sorts? Or rather the thought of new life with the ones you love? By some fate, this stage of life had never come for me and might never.

I was lost. Every item surrounding me constantly reminded me of what I had lost and would never get back. What gave me my security and bearings before was now a constant burning and aching thorn in my side. I made the decision. I put everything in order. I decided to sell everything I owned, except for a few small personal items and a few simple outfits that I put into my one wooden trunk. I made a considerable amount of profit, but to me it meant nothing. I traveled from one train station to the next and visited several hotels throughout Europe. I saw many places I had never seen before and they amazed me. I spent most of my money on useless, frivolous things. After a few years, the splendor was lost to the realization that no matter where I went, people were all the same. Whatever relationships I would make would not last due to my constant traveling, for if I stayed, I would have to let go of them eventually anyway.

I made the decision to take a boat and move to the East Coast in America. Manhattan was a place where there were enough faces, I could disappear. It was also a place filled with the new and upcoming, so nothing stayed boring for very long. I continued to move from place to place, but I always came back to living in the boroughs of New York. I made very few relationships and was careful never to mention my past to anyone. I buried my heart deeper in the grave back at home than ever before. Over time, no choice seemed to matter. The changes around me—from dirt roads and drawn carriages to paved roads and automobiles; small family-owned storefronts to monstrous steel skyscrapers; factories with child labor to labor laws and structured school systems—none of it changed the human condition bred in every new generation.

2

Last Tuesday I was sitting in the coffee shop where I visit a few times a week. The coffee shop is located at the bottom of a mid-rise building with apartments above. The family who runs it put a collection of different types of furniture, from plushy couches and armchairs to mismatched wooden tables and chairs, in their shop. They also hung obscure paintings on the walls from different local artists with the costs listed below each one. The smell of the beans beckons people in from the street.

I was sitting at one of the two-seater small wooden tables by the window. I stirred two sugar packets into my coffee with a wooden stir stick. There was a middle-aged man grabbing his order from the counter. He wore a hoodie, with the hood covering his head, and sweatpants as well as athletic shoes. To my surprise he came over and sat at my table across from me. He pulled the hood back from his head. His face seemed to glow, and there was something like sparks in his eyes. The sparks made his irises light up. There was a radiance coming from him that was awesome but also terrifying. No one else in the coffee shop seemed to notice.

"Eliza," the man said as a greeting.

Fear struck through me at the thought of a stranger

knowing my name. Was he following me?

"You do not need to be afraid. I know you have lived many years, about two hundred to be exact."

"What?" I sat dumbfounded.

"I know about your husband, Edmund, and your six children. I also know how much you miss them."

My mind must have been messing with me. Had I heard him correctly?

"Over the years you had nightmares of losing them. Then you did. You always questioned why you were the one who survived." He gave me an empathetic smile.

"Who are you?" I said in a trembling voice unlike my own. I felt myself becoming light-headed, as if I would fall out of my seat at any moment. How could anyone possibly know this much about my life? I never told anyone about the nightmares either. It was as if he could see into myself deeper than I ever could.

"You can say I am a messenger," he answered without breaking my glance. "There is a job I need you to do. It is very important."

The man handed me a receipt with words written on the back of it. What did the words mean? He told me where I would go. There would be a mysterious stranger I would meet. I was instructed when to say the phrases written on the paper. The messenger emphasized the importance of memorizing them beforehand. I tried to take in what he was saying but could not grasp the weight of its meaning and became overwhelmed.

"What does this have to do with me?" I asked him, still confused.

"I know not everything makes sense now. The important part is following through," he said; then he walked out of the coffee shop.

I sat for several minutes not knowing what had just happened. Who was this so-called messenger? How did he know my life story? I could not sort out the questions piling up in my mind. My only certainty was there were too many coincidences in his words for me not to do what he had said.

I look into the eyes of the man with the bomb. They glow, almost like those of the man who called himself a messenger, but then turn to a deep black. The darkness covers his eyes entirely. I want to scream but instead swallow and try to keep my mind focused. My shaking hands pull the receipt from my jacket pocket where I had left it last Tuesday. I know I was supposed to memorize it but can't help but second-guess myself now. Would it matter if I missed a single word? It might. The man studies me as I reread the two phrases over a couple times. I look around, then mutter the first phrase the messenger had given me.

"Open my eyes and allow me to see the truth behind the inner movements of every life."

All at once I am as light as a balloon drifting upward let go by some small child. There is an absence of gravity pressing down my shoulders, and I am more aware and alive than before. I forget my everyday worries, like what I will make for dinner tonight, or which bill I have to pay soon, or all the choices I wish I could remake. There is only here and now. I lose all sense of time. Where has the so-called messenger from the coffee shop taken me with a few simple words? It is astonishing, but with a sense of new wonder rather than fear.

After only a moment, I stop rising and peer at my body standing below. The men and women are walking in the subway next to my body. They look like actors in a grainy, black-and-white film from the past, unaware of the life swirling around them. They are a dull, murky version of themselves in this new world laid on top of the old. Everything in this place is somehow intertwined with the old one and works in harmony with it, but is more vivid and crisp. A golden plane, like a terrain of golden shapes thread together as if connecting the two dimensions. It stretches as far as I can see.

There are new colors I have never seen, as if I was blind before and am now seeing them for the first time. I am only a grain of sand in an endless ocean. Balls of light and dark energy whiz past me, leaving wisps of energy flowing behind them. The bright orbs of light have gold surrounding them, their wisps like lightning, and the dark ones have centers resembling dark smoke with tendrilled wisps like ink flowing through water. The wisped creatures whisper inaudible words into the ears of the people in the subway below. They appear to be tackling each other, fighting for control over the people they're trying to prompt.

A group of the orbs leaves my view. Anxiety spreads through me. One of the dark creatures has wrapped itself around the neck and head of the man with the bomb, its legs like vines of ivy encapsulating every surface it touches. It lets out a shrill, inhuman cackle giving me an edge-of-the-cliff teetering in my chest. I sink a bit, as if my spirit wishes to return to my body. It would be easy to give up and run away, but the messenger sounded serious when he said he needed this job carried out. This is probably the moment the messenger was referring to when he said I should recite the second phrase. I don't have access to the receipt at this point. I must remember it.

"In the name of the Mighty One"—I pause, trying to focus—"you will leave this place and enter . . . the Forlorn."

I recite these words to the wretched creature whose legs are grabbing at the bomber's neck. My voice reverberates in this otherworldly dimension. There is a loud screech of despair and defeat. The spindled limbs of the dark creature disperse like a thousand black spiders, and the smoke in its center dissolves until there is nothing left. A few feet from where I am, other dark creatures also dissolve while some remain in the distance much farther away.

I am heavy again and regain the mental fuzziness of everyday life. The familiar weight and restlessness of my normal self returns. The man in front of me no longer has a blank expression nor does he still have the dark glare, but he is

11

brought to his knees in his disorientation. He looks around as if not remembering how he got here. He glances up at me before looking down at the bomb on his chest. His trembling hands scramble to deactivate the bomb before he zips up his jacket and bolts out of view.

My hands are shaking, and my knees are moments from buckling. I take in deep breaths. I sit down on a nearby bench to collect myself. Would someone else have been able to stop him if I had not been here? People continue to come and go, unaware of the potential tragedy. The images of what could have happened play over and over in my mind.

What is it I have just experienced? How can this be explained? I can't even wrap my mind around it. The logical part of me wants to chase it away, saying it was only a dream or I probably ingested something I shouldn't have. But neither of these things is true. It all happened the way the messenger said it would. What will he say if I ever get the chance to confront him about it? It makes sense why he was vague in his instructions. He gave me just enough to compel me to follow through and find out what he'd meant but not too much to scare me away. I can't imagine this is the end of it. Knowing all he does about my history and my family, there must be more. Would this messenger be able to help interpret the layers of myself I have tried to comprehend for so many years?

3

It is a bright Sunday morning. These are the days I usually take my coffee and pastry to go so I can eat outside. It is very rare to get a weekend day off, but Craig was willing to fill in for me today. He asked if I was going on a trip, and I awkwardly looked back at him in silence, unable to explain I was only planning to people-watch at the local park. Some days the monotony of putting clothing back on racks is a welcome distraction, but other days it is isolating and mind-numbingly boring.

I watch the mother pushing her twins in a stroller with an older child, walking alongside, who's making one of them cry. There is an old man with his large dog looking more tired and worn down than he does. There is an ice-cream man pushing his cart with children flocking toward him. The crowd has all ages and temperaments, and pigeons nearby are picking up their crumbs.

It has been a couple weeks since the subway incident. I have been jumpy ever since I saw the bomber and visited the spirit world. I want to enjoy the crowd, but I also wonder when I will be able to enter a crowd of people again without experiencing anxiety. I still wonder when, if ever, I will see the messenger again.

I close my eyes and take deep breaths, trying to focus on the warm sun on my skin. The image of the dark creature cackling in my direction invades my mind, and I can't make it leave. I force myself to remember the new colors I saw and how alive I felt in the strange world. I look over at the crowd of people, and I can almost imagine the dark and light orbs, nudging people along without them being aware. How was the man with the bomb so influenced by the dark that he was willing to blow up a subway and take his own life?

I give the rest of my pastry to the pigeons cooing beneath me and then stand up to throw away my coffee cup in the trash can. I stand under the shade of a large oak tree, watching the crowd. I stand by a saxophone player who is sitting on the edge of one of the benches. He is playing a jazzy song and has his case open on the bench next to him. It has been filled with dollar bills and spare change. He is wearing a dirty and tattered peacoat and scuffed-up dress shoes. The man appears to be homeless or from a poorer area of town. He looks up from beneath his fedora.

The musician's eyes are glowing as he looks at me. I recognize the bright rim in his eyes. The glow has a heart-piercing sort of effect. It is the same way the man in the subway looked at me. His eyes become a deep well of darkness, the black completely filling in his eyes with no difference between pupil, iris, and cornea. The shadows seem to grow on his face as well as over his menacing smile. Goose bumps run up my back, but my feet remain planted. He stops playing. He continues to look at me. I wipe my clammy hands on my jeans, trying not to freak out.

"Hello, Eliza," he says in a hissing whisper.

This man is a stranger. How does he know my name? Stepping backward, I am able to get my feet moving again. I take off in a mad dash with my small purse bouncing beneath my arm and my boots propelling myself as fast as they can across the pavement. I struggle to catch my breath. I make it several blocks, not looking back, passing people and countless vehicles. I hop up the steps two at a time to my second-floor apartment studio. I jumble around in my purse and finally find my keys, nearly dropping them. I struggle to get my key into the keyhole. I open the door and slam it behind me. I lock the dead bolt and crumble to the floor, desperate to get control of my breath.

4

I slowly open my eyes when my alarm goes off, and I pull down my covers. I have not changed out of my clothes from the day before. My black cat, Cosmo, gives me a dirty look with his ears pulled back until I turn my alarm off. I spent the rest of yesterday watching TV under my covers and eating ramen, with all the blinds closed. I go over to the window and take a peep between the blinds. I only see a few people passing by, none of whom is the man I had seen yesterday. I groan. My head must be stuffed with cotton balls. Although I slept quite a lot, it didn't make a difference because for most of it I was tossing turning under my sheets. I look at my clock—I have work in about a half an hour—and I scramble to find a new outfit to change into. Before leaving, I throw a new outfit on and stuff down a breakfast bar.

The bell attached to the storefront door rings as I open the door. I have been working at this boutique for about three years now and am still not used to the stuffy smell inside. Change the carpeting and paint all you want; the old building has been around a long time. The boutique is sandwiched in between stores on either side and has several floors of apartments above it. There are large front windows looking in to reveal the round racks of clothing on the right as well as racks on the wall. The front desk is to the left and has an old-fashioned register with magazines and knickknacks on top.

I walk to the back room to stash my purse in a cubby and put my name tag on. There are piles of boxes and a small employee table with a microwave on top and a chair underneath. The table has wrappers and soda stains on it, and the microwave looks as grimy as ever with a hundred fingerprints. There's nothing to make employees feel appreciated like putting them in the presence of fire hazards. I let out a sigh and walk out.

I'm glad to see Ashley is here today and not our manager. She is about eighteen by my guess. Her dark hair is in a ponytail on the top of her head with her hair pouring down like a fountain. She is wearing high-waisted jeans and a colorful red-and-yellow off-the-shoulder crop top covered in large flowers. Her diamond knockoff earrings are massive and her makeup is thick. Ashley is bent over, leaning on her elbows, with her head craned over an open magazine on the desk while she is blowing bubbles with her gum. She looks up and says, "Hi, girl!" I give a small wave gesture in response. She has a little too much pep for my taste, but I would take it any day over working with Mr. Hardy.

Mr. Hardy is an older man and was actually happy when he hired me three years ago. He set up the store himself and named it "Sheila's Boutique" after his wife. When he ended up not making much profit (according to Mr. Hardy's claims), she started dating a younger man and filed for separation. Their ongoing divorce battle has had a toll on him these past few years. Many employees have come and gone, and Mr. Hardy will just calculate his profits in his books with the expression of a sad old bulldog plastered on his face.

I look at the go-back rack piled up from yesterday with the clothing people didn't want. Apparently, whoever was working yesterday was too lazy to do it themselves. I sort through the clothes and start placing them back on their racks. I half listen to Ashley talking and occasionally chime in with an "uh-huh" or a "yeah." Ashley first talks about an unlikely celebrity

17

couple, two people I don't know and don't care about, and then goes on about the order of clothing Mr. Hardy made. Ever since Mr. Hardy's divorce case has ramped up, the clothing he has picked is frumpier than ever and Ashley never fails to comment on it. I can't help but agree with Ashley. It's as if Mr. Hardy is picking out what he wishes Sheila would wear so as not to draw any male attention; either that or, due to his laziness, the latest fashion trends elude him.

A few hours pass with the occasional customer here and there and small talk being passed between Ashley and me once in a while. I go to the back room to clean the horribly sticky employee table. I wash my hands and enter the front room. Ashley is giving me a strange sideways glance with a stiff, uneasy look about her. I expect her to say something, but she stays quiet as I come closer to the front desk.

I look over and see the jazz man from yesterday. He peers up at me from behind the tall clothing rack and gives me a menacing golden-toothed smile. He is no longer shuffling through the clothing pretending to look for an item; now he is looking at Ashley and me straight in the eyes. He paces back and forth between the racks, waiting for us to move.

I try to brace myself for whatever will come next. I stand close to Ashley. Will the messenger appear and save us? Would he want me to do something, or do I wait for an intervention? Should we call the police? He hasn't really done anything to warrant a call. There is a standoff between us and the jazz man for several moments with uneasy glances among the three of us. We have had a few instances in the past of confused homeless people coming into the store, but they were persuaded to leave when they were not willing to buy anything.

Stepping out from behind the front desk, I plant myself in between the man and Ashley. Even though I haven't known Ashley for very long, I would still feel horrible if something happened to her. For a moment I recite in my head the words the messenger told me. If I don't do it now, the man might try to kill us both. His eyes are now totally black. He is not looking to make peace or leave anytime soon.

18

"Open my eyes and allow me to see the truth behind the inner movements of every life," I announce.

I rise above my body like I did the other day in the subway. I enter the crisp and clearer world once again. The creatures of gold and those of smoke are tackling each other and whizzing around above the people walking on the street. The jazz man's head is encased by the wisps of one of the dark forces, whose tendrils pulsate around him, threatening to cover more of the man. The dark creature grows taller, morphing into a monstrous-looking beast with several sets of moth-like wings, spider-like legs, and three heads having multiple eyes on each one. It has the tendrils coming from its pincers and legs. The beast fills up the room.

"In the name . . ."—my voice catches—"of the . . ." I freeze in terror unable to finish the sentence.

The tendrils from its giant pincers wrap around the neck of my body below in the physical world, and I somehow sense the pain. The weight of the fear pushes my spirit back into my body. I gasp in pain and put my hands around my throat. I drop to my knees and then collapse as I drift off.

It was 1878 and I had spent the past few weeks tending to Edmund's health by his bedside. A few months ago I had noticed he was slowing down and was unable to do what he used to. Even short walks were laborious for him, and he had to take breaks no matter what tasks he tried to complete. He did what work he could from home, but then had to discontinue work indefinitely. After what felt like a short amount of time, he was kept in bed each day. The doctor looked at his swollen ankles and said his illness was "dropsy," but it was what I would later recognize as heart failure.

I stood in my bedroom watching the leaves fall from the trees. I wore my black dress and veil I had worn several times already. I thought I had a few more years with him, but it was over. His hair had turned white many years ago, and he developed a slight curve in his back, but his eyes would still sparkle when he looked at me. Whenever I held my head low, he would put his hand in mine for encouragement. He was the first one to know my secret, and he held me steady despite my hopelessness and insecurities throughout our forty-two years together. Edmund was firm in his faithfulness to me and our family.

The shuffle of the staff echoed through our house. This would be the last look out any of the windows for several weeks after they closed all the curtains. The staff were also assigned the task of stopping the clocks, covering the mirrors and dressing the front door with a wreath as a sign of our mourning. Edmund's room was to be adorned with lilies and candles while his body would wait in his bed during his wake period.

I could not enter his bedroom and gaze at his pale face. It would remind me that every conversation between us had already been made. I wanted to remember Edmund as the kind, gracious man I had come to know and not contemplate the person I would become without him. I had spent so many years with his support and wise counsel, so it seemed impossible to go on without him. A vein of fear crept its way into my every thought. The world felt very large when I imagined facing future struggles without him.

No one could understand my grief. Those who worked in our house were told I was his great-niece who was willed the estate. For many years I had lived out this identity. Once we had changed our staff, I became Edmund's great-niece so no one would be suspicious of my unchanging appearance. Our children knew, because there was no way around it. We made them swear to never tell anyone, even their children. My grandchildren viewed me more as a peer. They tried to visit me when they could, but they had their own lives. Disease and devastations would take them away in the years after. Edmund's loss reminded me that one day soon they would also be gone. The anxiety in me increased each day, knowing I would be the last one left.

5

The short, coarse carpet presses up against my cheek, and I smell the griminess of every shoe that has walked into the boutique. I blink a few times. My body is so heavy. I move my limbs while Ashley is bent over me on her knees with a look of concern on her face. She helps me to my feet and sits me on the stool behind the front counter.

"Hold on," she says and then runs to the back room. I grab my neck and start coughing. A terrible pain comes from my neck, and my knees are sore from the fall. I wonder if this wisped creature has the ability to damage me beyond repair. It definitely contains the strength to cause immense pain. I go to the employee bathroom and see the purple ring around my neck in the mirror. Usually my body only takes a few minutes or hours to heal a scrape, depending on how bad it is, but this could take at least a day to go away completely.

"Come on, let's go," Ashley says, clinging to her purse. "I'm sure Mr. Hardy won't notice if we're gone for a few hours as long as we make sure to lock everything up."

I nod and grab my purse from the back room. Ashley puts up the closed sign and locks the front door.

We start walking down the street. "Don't worry, I only live about two blocks from here." She smiles but I can tell she is concerned. I can only imagine what she thinks happened. I know I don't understand it.

She unlocks the front door to her apartment. She also lives in a walk-up apartment, but hers is a bit shabbier than mine. Ashley apologizes for the mess and explains her mom is at work and her little sister is at school. She motions for me to sit on the couch, and I sink into it. The couch is ratty and old, similar to the rest of the mismatched furniture. Besides the large TV, almost every furnished item looks like it has been plucked from a cheap garage sale. There are dirty socks on the floor and a few stacks of paper and some glasses and bowls left out. Ashley passes me an ice pack, and I put it on my neck.

I turn my head to a rack of clothing behind the couch, hoping for a distraction from my burning neck. The rack is freestanding and consists of a bar held by two vertical poles on wheels on either end. One end of the rack holds several completed outfits, while on the other end hang a few half-finished ones. Most of them are bright patterns, similar to those Ashley wears to work. There is a small table with a sewing machine on it next to a stack of fabrics. Ashley takes away a few of the dishes to the kitchen before coming back to sit on the couch.

"Did you make those?" I croak as I motion to the rack. I struggle not to cough too much.

Ashley perks up. "Yeah, there is something about designing clothes . . . something about it I just love. I started it a few years ago just as a hobby. And now I can't see myself doing anything else."

"Wow, cool. Definitely better than retail."

"One day I want to go to a fashion school. I want a real job in fashion, not retail. But New York is so expensive when it comes to anything."

"I'm sure you will find a way," I say, trying to be encouraging.

"Thanks. There are other more important things that have to come first. My mom and sister couldn't survive without me." She looks around.

I'm not certain of what her situation is but gather she helps her mom keep the apartment and pay the bills. Their apartment is only a one-bedroom apartment for the three of them. Someone probably sleeps on the couch. Her younger sister must be considerably younger, judging by the Barbies and notebooks lying around.

"Let me see your neck," she says as she grabs for the ice pack. She almost grimaces as if sensing my pain. "It looks pretty bad." Ashley places her hands over the marks on my neck, and a warm tingling forms on my skin. The pain is somehow gone.

"How did you . . . ?" I stumble over my words. I run my hands over my neck. Still no pain.

"I think I saw something . . . in the boutique, I mean. You said something, and you were just standing there with a blank expression on your face. The man's eyes were totally black. I didn't know what I should do. I started to see the dark circle form around your neck, and before I knew it, your feet were starting to lift off the ground. But the man was still on the other side of the room."

My hands are getting clammy. Is it okay she knows about this other world? How much should I tell her? Can I trust her? Maybe if the messenger had told me more about my situation, I would now know how to go about all this. The messenger was absent when I needed him the most. I hope I see him again so I can force him to explain himself. As for Ashley, I have to take my chances with talking to her about this strange world revealed to me. There's something different about her too, it seems. How was she able to heal me so fast?

"There is this other place. It affects what happens here in our world. I don't know if it will make sense or not. I still don't know a lot about it." I pause, assessing her reaction. She has a calm demeanor, so I take a deep breath and continue. "There are pieces of darkness and light influencing what people do. The darkness seems to take over some people more than others and makes them do horrible things. There are constant battles we don't even see."

"Do you mean like some sort of spirit world?" Ashley asks.

"Yeah, I guess so." I expect her to tell me I am crazy.

"I met a man yesterday in the subway who told me you would need my help. He told me to stay close. I don't know how he knew all the information he did about me. It was really strange. I didn't know what help you would need, but it seemed pretty important."

"Did you get the name of this man?"

"No, he just called himself the messenger."

6

I'm sitting in one of my favorite comfy chairs looking out the coffee shop windows. The sun still wouldn't be up by now even if the sky was clear enough to see it. Such a lazy, gloomy morning—perfect day to skip out on work. Customers headed to work come in beforehand to get their coffee to go. People shake their umbrellas out and stomp their boots on the mat on their way in. I pull up my jacket around myself and slump further down in my chair. I can still almost feel the tight grip around my neck, and shudder. While I am physically healed, I know I am far from mentally okay.

Ashley called me a cab yesterday and encouraged me to take today off. I drink my coffee, glad I called in sick this morning. It's a lot to process. There is no way I would be able to work with how distracted I feel. What if the man comes back? I know I can't hide forever. I don't know how long he will continue to follow me, and I won't be able to take any more sick days with how expensive rent is. I'll try to see if I can make it up with overtime later.

At this point my mocha is getting lukewarm. Maybe if I drink it more slowly, it will give the messenger more time to show up. I can't be sure he will, but I figure it is worth trying, especially since this is where we first met. I tend to avoid confrontations, but this is something needing to be addressed. A part of me wants to see the expression on his face when I ask him where he was when I was attacked. Did he leave me alone just to have me suffer? Out of everyone, he should have been there or sent for rescue. I wonder how long he will let me flounder with these encounters until he intervenes.

The messenger is grabbing his drink from the counter. I lower my head as he sits in the chair next to mine. Anger and frustration well up inside me. We sit a while before either of us says anything, and I can't bring myself to look into his eyes. After all I have said to him in my head, I am now not sure where to start.

"I know you are upset," he says without alarm.

"An understatement, for sure," I say as I cross my arms and roll my eyes.

"There were certain things not told to you for a reason."

"Oh, really? Reasons like waiting around for me to fail?" I retort with a thick sarcasm.

"It was a test to see what you would do, how you would behave. Not for us, but for yourself. You were first so afraid you ran back to your apartment—"

"And for good reason too," I said, cutting him off.

"But then you confronted him, even despite your fears," he continues, unfazed.

"But I lost! He almost choked me! I know I have lived a long time and come back strong from most things but . . . who knows?"

"We were there to push him back before he could do any more harm. This encounter showed you a small part of what you are to stand up against in the future. There will be times when you want to run and hide, but the enemy is out there wanting to destroy people. Choosing not to fight will also be an option."

My anger begins to settle as my curiosity takes over. These could be pieces to the answers I have been looking for. I must make the most of my time with the messenger. What else will he be willing to tell me? Will I be able to decipher the underlying meaning in his words?

"What is the dark creature I saw in the boutique?" The jazz man's glowing eyes turning to black is imprinted in my memory. I shudder.

"He is who they call Levizar. He is the region leader over all the tormentors and tempters in this area. All the dark spirits you have seen so far in our world follow him. The region leaders are promoted above these evil spirits and have poured out a lot of blood and grief to be in their kind of power. They are commanded by the Ruler of Darkness to destroy the most in the worst ways possible in return for a higher ranking. The region leaders are more powerful and have to be weakened to be sent to the Forlorn."

"How are they weakened?"

"The region leaders can't be sent to the Forlorn, unless they have many of those under them taken out first. If this is not done first, the phrase I gave you will not work."

"What is the Forlorn?"

"The Forlorn is a dark place where all the cursed spirits will eventually go. Their main goal is to get humans to be with them there as well. They not only want people to suffer here on earth but permanently after they pass away. These people we call the inconsolables. At some point, there is no escaping it." The messenger wears a solemn look as he says this part.

"You are the ones keeping back the cursed spirits?"

"Yes, some of this is what you saw in the spirit world. The Mighty One gives direction to the messengers, and the messengers tell the guardians where to go in order to have the most positive result. Some messengers appear as human for some special orders. Tormentors and tempters are not strong enough to do this and have to take over human bodies. We have kept many potential tragedies from happening by delaying the tormentors and tempters."

"But how do the cursed spirits take over people?"

"People were designed to be good but are broken. They fall into their own unhealthy patterns and then willingly follow them, causing their hearts to turn cold and stubborn. People

28

embrace pride instead of humility, and this allows the cursed spirits to take control. They refuse to accept they are broken and in need of a change. People then continue to take what is not theirs, lie to themselves and others, and kill to get what they want. If they ask for the grace they need, it will be given to them. So many refuse and end up lost forever. If their hearts are examined and are shown to have a real change, they don't have to fear the Forlorn. They are protected after this point. They are given different gifts to help destroy the darkness of the world. Some see their abilities right after their hearts have passed the testing, others have theirs delayed for different reasons. Others choose to hide what it is they can do, due to fear or apathy, and waste it."

"So . . . my ability to make the dark spirits leave is one of them? Why can't I remember when my heart was tested?" The more the messenger speaks to me, the more questions pile up in my mind.

The messenger nods. "You were very young when it happened. There will be a time when you will remember it."

"What about having to leave my family behind? Is it really necessary I lived a full two hundred years before reaching this point? What does it have to do with anything?" I may never fully understand anything. This thought leaves me flustered.

"There will be a correct time for everything, nothing is accidental. One day you will see and understand. Your ability to banish the cursed spirits has been revealed in this time where people are no longer softening their hearts. When a cursed spirit has taken them over, the need to change is no longer seen by them. They are blind to the desperation of their soul. We, the messengers, the guardians, and the Mighty One, have together been prompting you and protecting you all along. You were never alone."

"How does this involve me?"

"We need you to give them an opportunity for another chance, Eliza. You must continue to face this evil again and again with courage. Keep close to those in your circle. At times it will require a lot of sacrifice and risk. Many tempters and tormentors must be taken down before you face Levizar again."

I open my mouth to speak again, not sure what I might ask, when the messenger gets up and walks away. I look away for a second and back, and he is gone. It's as if he vanished into the air. I imagine he disappeared in the spirit world to deliver his next message. I sit dumbfounded, unable to move from my chair.

The messenger has made it clear my involvement will include more than the one task he gave me. There has been a plan for me all along. It is hard to believe everything going on around me is in some way connected to this other world. Only a few months ago I was not even aware of its existence. Even though I should be grateful with the amount of answers the messenger was able to give me, I am intimidated by the importance of my every action. What other challenges will I be forced to overcome? I am comfortable with staying hidden for my own protection like I have been used to for years. It has left me without any close connections, but it is always safer. I will now be forced to take some risks. Who will I become dealing with this new realm? I look around the coffee shop at people for hours, studying their mundane behaviors while my mind spins.

It was 1868 and I was a few weeks older than fifty. The two large marble women towered above me from the top of the mausoleum, holding out their arms. Most of the trees had lost their leaves, and a morning frost covered the ground. I shivered as a gust of wind blew on my neck. There was always something unsettling about this place which left me with an eerie feeling. Maybe it was because of the memories surrounding it. Saying good-bye to our young daughter Scarlet was one of the hardest moments Edmund and I had to get through. I wrapped my shawl tighter around my shoulders, unable to keep myself warm.

I took the iron key from my dress pocket and put it in the keyhole of the cast-iron doors. I walked inside as the rain started to fall on my back. Squinting my eyes, I struggled to adjust my eyes to poor lighting inside. The only lighting present was from the faint sunlight making its way through the clouds and past the doorway. I reached out my gloved hand and ran my fingers over the marble until I felt the engraved lettering:

"Elizabeth "Eliza" Hart, 1818–1868, beloved sister, daughter, and wife."

It was surreal seeing my own name in front of me. Would I ever have a real grave site someday? I knew I could no longer continue pretending I was middle-aged when I looked like I was twenty. It was a fresh start, in a way. I could not help but wonder if I would be able to make my new identity believable. I had spent hours in my head rehearsing what I would say to anyone who questioned my authenticity. I was now considered to be Edmund's great-niece. He would tell others my husband had died and I had no one to look after me. It was his responsibility as the wealthy relative to support me.

I was tired of playing the part of an actress. Before we faked my death, I would have to fix my hair and makeup every morning so not even my maid who helped me dress would notice my youthful appearance. It began to take more effort than it was worth. I was afraid my disguises would not work for much longer. It was also taking its toll on me.

I had cried in Edmund's embrace over a month prior after a dinner party we had hosted. It took me several hours of preparation and an evening of acting for people we hardly liked. I never liked the meaningless chitchat of pretending to be an old woman. It was as if I had to make something on my body pretend to ache to appease our older guests with their troubles. Even if my body really was fifty, I had doubted I would put up as much of a fuss as they had. If these women were not complaining about their bodies, they were certainly complaining about someone else. Did I hear about so-and-so's failing marriage? What about their wayward child? I refused to consume their gossip and always tried to change the subject. There were certain guests my husband was obliged to invite over for business or social reasons. I could not bear it any longer. I would have no problems with hiding in my room until they all left if they thought of me dead. Edmund noticed my grief and suggested my own funeral should be planned. We knew our butler had plans of retiring soon, so we took it as the perfect opportunity to replace our staff after my identity change. The new workers would not be able to identify me as Edmund's wife.

Staring at my name, I knew there would be fewer restrictions in some ways, but more in others. If I wanted to go to town, I would dress myself as a mourner with a veil covering my face. For the most part, I would be kept inside our home without many guests who would be allowed to visit. Even when Edmund announced my death to our household, I had to sit in my locked room. The former staff members were not allowed to enter, but Edmund made his way into my room when no one was looking to bring me food or a book to entertain myself.

After a few minutes, I stepped outside the mausoleum and into the rain, which was falling at a steady pace. I closed the iron doors and locked them shut. Edmund had told me how people came to our house to mourn over my coffin and say their last words. There were some whom I cared about and grieved that I would no longer be able to see. I would be leaving them and my other self behind. Would I be able to figure out how to handle this new life? While the thought of embracing my new identity looked promising, it was also daunting. I would always enjoy the company of my family in my home while they were with me, but I was not sure if I was equipped when it came to interacting as a great-niece rather than a wife and mother.

7

I slide into the red-cushioned booth with my one hand balancing my tray. I look down at my pizza slice and the pools of grease sitting on the pieces of pepperoni. Holding up my slice to let some of the grease drop off, I look up at Ashley who is helping her sister Carmen into the other side of the booth. Ashley invited me to come to dinner with her after our shift. At work Ashley mentioned something about having to watch Carmen while we ate because she didn't want to pay the babysitter extra to work this late. I said I didn't mind. Carmen is eight years old and full of energy. Carmen sits with her legs folded under her and her elbows propped up on the table as she takes her first bite, sound effects and all.

It has been a long, pretty overwhelming work week, even for retail standards, but somehow we are both not scheduled for tomorrow, which is Friday. Today was the only other day of the week Ashley and I worked together since the incident on Monday. We didn't talk much because of the customers who needed our help. There was one woman in particular who was pretty angry and took everything personally. She insisted on finding a specific blouse since she was certain it would be the only gift to appease her niece. The lady was heavyset in a dress suit and wore a foul-smelling perfume like vinegar and moth balls put together. She reeked like a typical Sheila's Boutique customer.

The boutique is quite small, but it still took almost an hour to find what she was looking for. Our inventory is not exactly organized like it should be because Mr. Hardy insists on not using much technology to run his business. After the lady finally left, there were more people than usual who came in and out. Ashley usually saves her magazines and her gossip for when there is a lull because there are no customers and almost every task has been managed. Ashley and I are grateful we finished out a work week without making too many customers unhappy and were able to keep our sanity. Ashley insisted on going out for a mini celebration. According to her, pizza counted as one.

We sit back in the booth, now working on eating our crusts. We both have aching feet from pacing circles around the store all day. There is an older couple in the booth next to us, but most of the customers are young college students, some wearing NYU apparel. I see Ashley eyeing them with what looks like envy. I recall her explaining how much she wishes she could afford to go to school. The students' conversations are loud and flirtatious, and about half of them are on their phones, swiping up on their social media of choice while barely talking to each other in person. I can tell Ashley is tired because she hasn't said much since we got our food.

I try to remember how long it has been since I have had any friendships or even someone I could rely on. I believe, so far, I can trust Ashley. She seems to be a genuine person. On the other hand, we haven't known each other very long. If I am going to trust someone, I have to have a good reason. Not everyone will earn my trust. I figure, Ashley did heal my neck and the messenger did find and talk with her. She did put herself out there by presenting her healing ability. Is she somehow like me when it comes to her healing? The messenger had told me there were others with abilities. If the messenger trusts her enough to give her direction, then I should be able to confide in her.

"I saw the messenger yesterday," I tell Ashley.

"Oh, yeah? What did he say?"

"He said something about people having their hearts examined or tested. If they pass, they are given certain abilities. Do you remember having anything like this happen to you?"

Ashley looks off into the distance and furrows her brow. She shakes her head. "What is it exactly?"

"He said it is a point where you give up control of your life, or your pride, and ask to be saved from your own brokenness."

"Hmm . . . no, I can't remember."

"When you placed your hands on my neck . . . and it healed . . . it felt like you had done it before. Is that right?" I ask Ashley.

"I have had my healing power for quite a while now."

"My sister heals a little fast, that's all!" Carmen chimes in with alarm.

Ashley laughs at her. "It's okay, Carmen. We can tell her our secret." Carmen relaxes a bit.

Ashley continues, "When I was little, I didn't think anything of it. My scrapes would only last a few minutes before going away. It took me a few years to realize not everyone could do this. Back when we lived in our house as a family, we had this cat named Hershey. It would follow me everywhere. One day there was a car coming down our street so fast it didn't even slow down for Hershey. He ended up being pushed under the tires of the car. The jerk didn't even stop or anything."

I nod, my eyes getting big.

"Hershey was still alive, but his legs were twisted in a sick and unnatural way. He was still breathing, but there was no way he would be able to walk. I picked him up and placed him on the sidewalk. I stroked his fur, crying over him. A warmth came out of my hands. I opened my eyes and his legs were no longer twisted. He ran back into the yard like nothing had happened. I didn't know what to think."

"Wow, that's amazing." I stare at her with my mouth slightly gaping open.

"Yeah, well, he still died from old age a few years later. If I hadn't gotten to him in time, I probably wouldn't have been able to save him."

"Have you ever healed people . . . besides me, I mean?"

"Yeah, when my sister Carmen was little, I would heal her scrapes too." She sighs. "Sometimes she will get hurt on purpose just to see me heal her. Just little cuts, but it's annoying. For example, I have to keep her out of the kitchen," Ashley says as Carmen gives her a devious smile.

"That sounds rough." I wish I could tell her I once had siblings too, but I can never express this. It's hard enough to come up with a convincing back story without adding siblings. I'm intrigued by her ability to heal others and wonder how injured a person could be and still come back with her help.

We eat in silence, absorbing the flavors of our pizza. The jumbling conversations and the bright decorations bring life to the pizza place. Why do I choose heating up my food in my apartment over this? I'm glad Ashley feels she can confide in me. I hope one day I will be able to do the same. At this moment, it would seem like a great risk to tell anyone about my true life story. I must remember not to let my guard down too much, or I could be in real danger.

"Stop it. Sit down," Ashley snaps. Carmen went from hanging on the edge of the table to picking off the gum underneath it. Her caramel pigtails bounce up and down as her pizza sits half-eaten and probably cold on the top of the table. Ashley mutters something about the stupid babysitter always giving in to feeding Carmen snacks. Carmen reminds me of my daughter Scarlet when she was alive. Full of energy to the point of needing discipline.

"Sorry if she gets too loud." Ashley rolls her eyes, exasperated.

"It's okay." I give a half smile. Carmen bounces up on her knees on Ashley's side of the booth and rips off large bites of pizza, chewing with her mouth open. Ashley lets out a sigh, as if she has given up.

After Ashley and I finish our pizza, Ashley gets a look of excitement in her eyes. She tells me about a fashion contest she plans on entering. Ashley swipes through some images on her phone of her recent sketches, which she plans on making into clothing, and an image of a dress she finished sewing this week. I ask her a few more questions about the dress, but then she gets lost in showing me others' designs on her fashion boards online, and I feign interest as I struggle to pay attention. Carmen starts ripping at the crust of her pizza; she's leaning on her elbows while still sitting on her knees. Ashley gets sucked into her phone, and we are again sitting in silence with the laughter of the college students in the background.

A few students go outside. In a moment a few more follow them. A crowd of people is forming outside, looking at something I can't see from my seat. My curiosity is piqued. I say I will be right back and head outside alongside a few more individuals. At first I don't see what people are focused on, but then I look up.

There is a young woman across the street in sweats and a tank top standing on the railing of her fire escape with one hand clinging to the bottom of the steps above her. The sickly yellow streetlights illuminate the edges of her silhouette and cast dark shadows across her face. With her feet on the railing, she leans toward the edge, her head pointed toward the street three stories below. She extends her arm that is holding on to the bar above her but does not let go. The woman starts sobbing and puts her free hand over her mouth. The people below start to panic, frantically contemplating what they should do. One middle-aged man calls 911. I must have been standing outside for a few minutes because I suddenly see Ashley and Carmen next to me.

Ashley looks up and puts her hand over her mouth as she curses. Ashley pulls Carmen close to her. "Don't look."

"Look at what? I want to see!" Carmen's little head pokes up around Ashley's arms.

"Just . . . never mind. Here, do you want to play the game on my phone?" Carmen lets out a squeal of delight and yanks away Carmen's phone.

Ashley and I look up at the woman on the railing. My breath

catches. Is this another symptom of the conflicts arising in the spirit world? I can't be sure until I visit the other world again. This time there is no mysterious stranger with glowing eyes. The messenger didn't tell me anything about this happening. Would he want me to step out into the spirit world without his suggestion? My mind wanders to the jazz man in the boutique. The messenger said I was right in trying to confront him, even though he knew the jazz man was not weakened enough for me to banish him. My heart beats faster knowing if I go into the spirit world with my phrase, I might face the jazz man, or Levizar, again. Eventually, it is something I know I will have to do. I scan the crowd for him, and an uneasiness crawls up inside me. Will I ever really be ready? I attempt to steady my breathing in preparation.

I close my eyes and mutter the phrase to myself out loud in a whisper: "Open my eyes and allow me to see the truth behind the inner movements of every life."

I ascend as the heaviness leaves me again. The woman above is a dull color. There is a dark creature with its arms and legs around her shoulders. It lets out a small sound into her ear and pushes her back so she sways away from the building and closer to the street. It gives out a shrill cackle and continues to jab her back. Chills run up my spine, but I fight off the heaviness to sink away to my body. She won't be able to hold on much longer.

"In the name of the Mighty One, you will leave this place and enter the Forlorn."

My voice bounces off the different planes of this world. The cursed spirit and those near it let out shrieks and melt away. Guardians are circling around where the black ones were a few seconds ago, leaving behind trails of gold. I let the heaviness take me back, and everything seems foggy again.

The lady on the fire escape looks around as if she is confused. She gets down from the railing and stands on the fire escape platform. She falls onto her knees, sobbing harder than she was before. She stops and looks up. Her face has a faint glow. A few people in the crowd, also falling to their knees, have faces mirroring hers. Ashley and I give each other puzzled expressions. We wait a few moments in silence before Ashley says she has to get Carmen to bed. We part ways, and I walk to my apartment. I'm relieved I was able to chase off the cursed spirit without any conflict, but I am filled with curiosity over the glowing faces in the crowd.

8

I rock back and forth on my heels in front of the gelato shop where Ashley told me to meet her this afternoon. She texted me last night when I got home and asked me if I wanted to hang out today. I didn't tell her yesterday was a week's worth of socializing for me. I'm not sure if I even sound normal in most conversations, seeing how I spend most of my time by myself. I always tend to feel a bit awkward at best. Social interactions are not my strength. I decided to push these thoughts aside and agreed to meet her. It would be more entertaining hanging out with her than spending my whole day binge-watching my shows in my apartment like I usually do on my Saturdays off. It would also be interesting to see what her thoughts are on what happened last night with the woman and others with glowing faces.

Ashley is walking toward me in one of her off-the-shoulder bright floral tops and torn blue jeans. I wave, and her eyes lock onto mine as she spots me.

"Hey, girl. I wasn't sure if you would be awake when I texted you last night."

"Yeah, I am usually up pretty late."

As we make our way into the gelato shop, the bell on the door rings. Some college-aged guy comes out behind the counter looking like he would rather be anywhere else. Ashley picks the mango and I pick the strawberry flavor. After we receive our gelato and pay for it, we take it outside and start walking while we eat. I grimace as I begin to feel a brain freeze.

The sidewalk is different colors of gray, worn down, and unlevel. It's crowded with people fighting for room. The clouds are becoming much denser, and the wind is starting to pick up. The air is hanging thick with moisture. My phone clock tells me its later in the afternoon, even though it's hard to tell the time of day with the sun hidden. We dodge many people while trying to stay next to each other, and pass over a few large crosswalks at lighted intersections.

"Yesterday was really weird. Did you see people's faces glowing?" Ashley starts. I had wondered if she was going to bring it up.

"Yeah, I'm not sure why. Did the messenger say anything to you about it?"

She shakes her head. "Did you see anything in the spirit world like you did with the man in the store?" she asks.

"I saw one of those cursed spirits over the woman on the fire escape. I said the phrase the messenger told me, and it made him leave."

"I could tell something had happened. A few people even went to their knees."

"Yeah, it must be related, but I'm not sure how."

I'm not surprised Ashley doesn't know any more about it than I do, although it was worth a try asking her. I figure the messenger has to show up to one of us again soon. I'm hoping he can tell us more. There is a lot I still don't understand, not only about the spirit world but about myself.

Once the streetlight changes, we make our way over to the giant arch. The symbol of Washington Square Park towers over us. After many attempts, we find two seats next to each other on a bench. The park is alive with the different rhythms of street performers and the people who pass by to watch. I look around, a little anxious being back where I first encountered the jazz man, while Ashley seems to be delighted by the street performers. She points to a man who is juggling but can't help but dropping his balls every few seconds, apologizing profusely and then managing to find them all again. Ashley then shifts her focus to a man who is attempting to play a recorder with his nose.

"Oh no. Nah ah. I don't think so!" She gives me a look of disgust and then points. "They don't know it yet, but they need my help!"

It takes me a minute to realize she is appalled by his outfit and not by the playing-a-recorder-out-of-his-nose part. The man trying to play the recorder is wearing a plaid top with army-print cargo shorts. His socked feet stick out of his grimy sandals. Ashley takes a sketch pad and a pen out of her purse and starts drawing different fashion designs based on the ones she is seeing in real life. I smile to myself, trying to keep myself from laughing at her. There are some pretty hideous outfits out here, as well as horrendous performances.

A flash of movement comes up next to me, and my heart skips a beat, but I take a breath of relief when I turn my head to see it's only a man walking his dog. I don't see anyone who would be cause for alarm. I only see students, families, and couples. I look at the shadows underneath the bushes, as if the jazz man could be hiding there, but only see a squirrel scurry out of them. I wouldn't miss him if I saw him, right?

"Things have been really difficult with Carmen lately," Ashley says, interrupting my reverie. She keeps the pen moving across her page as she talks. "She has been acting out more and more."

"It didn't bother me. I—"

Ashley looks up at me, waiting for me to finish.

"It was still nice seeing her at the restaurant, I mean."

I almost didn't stop myself. I wanted to say I was used to it. But how could I say I was used to it, that I understood? What life experience would I use as a reference? Surely I could not tell her that at one point in my life I, in fact, had six kids myself. I don't look anywhere near that age for that to be a possibility. Even if I did make up a story about myself where I did have

42

kids, where would they be now? Would she believe that I am in such a dismal place that I don't want to see my children or am not allowed to? Instead, I just have to pretend I genuinely like children.

A light drizzle starts, and we both pull out umbrellas from our purses. She scrambles to put away her sketch pad before the rain ruins it. We both sit in silence on the bench watching others pull out their umbrellas and some performers packing up their instruments and others continuing to play in the rain.

"Yeah, Carmen is one of a kind. It's been really hard for her, though. Our dad left when she was really young. She was too young to remember him walking out on us. I never know what to say when she asks where our dad is. Or why he left. My mom transferred jobs to move out of Jersey so we could escape to Manhattan. We had to move to a tiny apartment, and now it's a struggle to get by . . ." I see her looking down at her boots and picking off the debris from them. She pulls a stray strand of hair back behind her ear. Ashley sniffles a bit but then looks up and smiles. "What about you? What's your story?"

Blood rushes from my face. I hope she doesn't notice. I have told my story to others before in bits and pieces but probably not in depth for a few years at least. This time it's different. I care about Ashley. Would I be able to lie to her?

"I grew up in England with my parents and family."

"Nice, I wouldn't have guessed. You barely sound like you have an accent."

"I acclimate well, I guess." In reality it has taken a while, around a hundred years of adjustments after my move from England. "I decided to move to New York to find a career here. Not much success yet, but we will see."

"Cool, what is it you want to do?"

"Don't know if I even have it figured out yet." I give a half smile.

"I know what you mean about the whole career thing." She pauses and lets out a chuckle. "So . . . in England do you really sit around and drink tea all day?"

"Um, something like that." I blush but am relieved she

43

didn't ask a more complicated question.

"Hey, it was just a joke." She nudges me with her elbow.

Ashley tells me about the first design she will be starting for her fashion contest. She mentions she still has to buy more fabrics before she can start. Our conversation turns from fashion to visiting the Met soon and taking a stroll through Central Park. We have spent our whole day without one mention of work—what a relief.

The rain has stopped, but I can see darker clouds pulling in with some thunder in the distance. When would I remember the heart testing that the messenger mentioned? Was there something else he hasn't told me yet? Families have left with their small children already, but there are still elderly couples, teenagers, and college students walking around. One teenage couple is kissing under their umbrella as if they are the only ones in the park. Only a few of the street performers remain.

My line of thought is broken when a scream rings out in the distance. The cry reverberates through the walkways of the park. More voices cry out in unison, joining the ones in the distance. The hairs on my neck stand up. Two teenage boys riding bikes are making their way through the park throwing rocks at people. Some of the rocks hit heads. There is an elderly woman on the ground with blood running down the side of her head. Many others are on the ground injured. The bicyclists make their way toward the street. I run out to them, trying not to waste any time. I rise up into the strange other world with the first phrase which I have completely memorized now. I yell out the second phrase until the cursed spirits over the teenagers disintegrate.

The heaviness from coming back into my body is a lot more than usual. I sit on the ground exhausted. Does my body not have enough energy to go into the spirit world multiple days in a row? I assumed it wouldn't affect me. I tuck in my legs toward my chest as I watch the guys fall from their bikes in their loss of coordination. One of them continues riding after he is able to pull himself up, but the other teenager is on his knees, looking upward with his face glowing. A few men,

44

women, and children are also looking up with glowing faces.

"Are you okay?" I see Ashley next to me.

"Yeah, I'm okay."

"Come on," she says, extending her hand to help me up before going over to the injured. I follow her, watching her put her hands onto people until they are healed. There is an elderly lady on the ground who looks confused, as well as a college-aged woman and a few other adults with less serious wounds. A few victims say something close to a thanks, but most are dumbfounded and in shock.

I inch toward the dark shadowed area where I was looking earlier. There must be something behind the bunching of trees between the two pathways. A chill comes over me. A broad-shouldered figure with a set of glowing eyes rises from the shadows. I pat Ashley's shoulder with more force than I intend to.

"Ouch! What is it?" She looks up from the young couple she is helping.

"It's time to go." I yank at the crook of her arm when she doesn't respond.

She gives me a glare.

"Now!" I say firmly.

Ashley senses my urgency but wears a baffled expression. She lets me pull her along until we are both running. I only hope we can get away in time. Why are the guardians not here to protect us? My legs become sore because of the long strides I take, but the adrenaline makes me not notice so much. A few times we cut off traffic, nearly getting hit, but we press on. We run up the stairs. I open my apartment door, and we run inside. I slam it behind us, locking the dead bolt.

9

I sit back on my couch with Ashley next to me. I begin to catch my breath after a few minutes. I'm not sure if we are really any safer in my apartment than out there, but it still gives me some sense of security. I am still uneasy knowing the jazz man can continue to surprise me again and again with little warning. I place my hands on my neck, remembering the fear of what I imagined were my last moments as he choked me. Ashley rubs her face and puts her head in her hands.

"What was that?" she asks, looking bewildered.

"You remember the man who came in on Monday?"

Her eyes begin to widen. "Did you see him?" Ashley says.

I nod. "He is still following me. I saw him in the park first . . . We saw him at work . . . and now at the park again."

"And you said . . . he has one of those things . . . following him?" she asks.

"Yeah, the messenger explained it to me more the day after the jazz man came into the boutique."

"What did he say?"

"People harden their hearts, and this allows those dark spirits, whom he calls tormentors and tempters, to take over. The one the jazz man has is different, though. More powerful. He is the leader of the weaker ones. They call him Levizar. The messenger said I can't get this spirit away from the man until I get rid of a lot of those under his control."

"Do you know how many?"

"No, he didn't say anything about it. And I don't know if he will. I'm guessing it's mostly in Manhattan, though. I do know by expelling these spirits people will be free to choose again. They will be able to see the need to soften their hearts. If they ask to be saved from their destructive patterns, they will pass their heart testing. Then they will be safe."

"What do you mean *safe?*"

"There is a place the messenger mentioned. The Forlorn, he called it. It's a dark place where the cursed spirits will all go one day, but they also want to bring people there too. Everyone's heart is tested at some point. If they pass, their souls will be safe from the Forlorn. Or so says the messenger."

"You said something in the pizza place about hearts being passed through a testing and gaining certain abilities. I can't remember this happening to me, but do you?" Ashley asks me.

I shake my head. "The messenger said I would remember . . . eventually. You can heal yourself and others, so you must have had one. And I can go into the spirit world and expel evil forces . . ." I leave out the part where I say how long I have been alive. Is this a part of my gift or just a curse? "The messenger said people are given these abilities to help out somehow."

Ashley gives me a confused expression and then looks down to the floor. "It's a lot to try to understand."

We sit in silence for a few minutes, deep in thought. My cat Cosmo hops up on the couch beside us, rubbing his face up against me. We both agree it is not safe to risk going out tonight. If anything, it will be a comfort to have someone's company. Ashley will just have to sleep on the pullout bed in the couch under my loft bed and then get her stuff early in the morning at her place before work. I also work tomorrow but not until the afternoon. Mr. Hardy insists on us being available at least one weekend day, and this weekend we both have the Sunday shift. I pull out a few blankets from my dresser while

Ashley pulls out the couch. She sits on the edge of it.

"The messenger . . . he told me you would need my help," Ashley starts, "but I didn't understand how at first. Now I'm thinking he means more than just the one time at work." Ashley takes the blankets from my arms.

"He also told me to stay close to those in my circle." I start laying out the blankets on the pullout bed. There must be others out there too.

"I don't mind sticking around to help out." Ashley finds my remote and turns on my TV. "It could be good to help people and stuff, right?"

"Yeah." I appreciate her positivity but am still shaken up on the inside.

I go to my kitchen and start heating up some water for the ramen. I apologize for not having anything else to cook, but Ashley says she doesn't mind. We start to watch some sitcoms while we eat on the pullout bed. Ashley starts laughing, and I struggle not to spill the broth all over. I can't help but laugh, but I'm laughing more at her contagious laughter than the show we are watching. My anxiety starts to melt away, and I'm grateful I don't feel alone.

I recall when I was around Ashley's age. It was 1836 and I had been introduced to Edmund a week earlier. My family had a relaxing day indoors, all of us preoccupied with our different hobbies. I was working on a line of poetry in my journal when I heard Anne and her parents pull up in their carriage. We would have them come over every Sunday afternoon to have tea with us in our guest parlor. I had been friends with Anne ever since we were little.

We all found our seats; mine was next to Anne's. Anne and I sat in silence as our parents discussed what would happen when King William passed away. Victoria was not of age yet, and if he had a sudden death, the throne would be passed to her mother, the Duchess of Kent. Victoria was the same age as I was. I couldn't imagine becoming royalty, much less queen. We finished our tea, and Anne and I were excused to go outside.

I led Anne through the wild brush and wildflowers down a small dirt path. We would often go this way, and we would see what small animals or rocks we could find. Anne talked about her trip to town the day before and what she wanted to get the next time she went. I tried to sound excited as she continued talking about the items she had seen. We came upon our favorite oak tree, where we would sit under its shade and where, when we were younger, we tried to make flower necklaces for each other.

Anne could sense I was more quiet than usual and asked me what was wrong. I started crying. I could no longer stop my tears from coming. I told her about Edmund coming to our home. I explained that my parents were looking to make a match for me soon and they wouldn't have invited him over if they were not serious. I felt I was still too young to be united with the person I would have to spend the rest of my life with. Anne put her arms around me in a tight embrace. She also couldn't believe my parents would try to find me someone so soon. I didn't tell her about my father's sickness and how he might not be with us much longer. I couldn't bring myself to say it because I didn't want to believe it was true.

10

As I walk into Sheila's Boutique, I notice Ashley and Craig have already started putting out the new inventory. It looks like they have been at it all morning. There are several boxes piled up at the back of the store. Carmen is also in the corner playing with her doll. Ashley gives me a quick "hey," then turns to look at a list and goes searching for a box in the pile. She crouches down to look at some of the labels on the sides of the boxes.

Ashley lets out a sigh. "They were supposed to do some of this last night. Mr. Hardy wanted us to work on it later tonight, but we will never get it all done by the time he comes in tomorrow if we wait." Craig is hanging up articles of clothing from the pile resting in the crook of his arm.

Craig hangs up the last top and says, "We can do it. No worries." He looks at me and smiles as I grab an armful of clothing from Ashley. Ashley looks up at the clock as if not hearing him.

"Can you start hanging these?" Ashley motions me to a box of hangers and another box of blouses. "It's just too much. It's bad enough they left this for us, but I'm stuck with babysitting duty too." Ashley mimics shooting herself in the head with her hand.

I laugh at her. "Really that bad, huh?"

"Nah, I'm just tired." Ashley wipes her forehead with the back of her arm and sits on the stool behind the counter.

"You can rest a minute while we take over."

To my surprise Carmen is calmer than any other time I have seen her. She is changing one of her dolls' outfits while sitting on the floor. She bounces the doll up and down, talking with animated expressions as if talking for the doll. I smile, reminded that my daughters did the same thing.

"These are the last of this box." I hand the blouses on hangers to Craig.

"Thanks! You are fast!" He gives me a goofy grin.

I have worked with Craig before, but we have never really talked much. I know he is in his early twenties even though he looks a couple years older. His eyes are hidden behind dark, thick frames, and the front part of his dark brown hair almost touches the top of his glasses. Craig reaches out with his lanky arms and grabs the hangers in one swoop with his large hand. He is considerably taller than I am and sometimes has to crouch to reach the lower rods on the wall while putting clothes in place. He is wearing a polo and khaki shorts. His athletic shoes look like they have been worn down over the past year or two.

Ashley opens a new box with many sizes of a blouse in varied colors. She now hands them to me as I put them on hangers. After several minutes, we all get into a rhythm, and before long we are working without having to think about what we're doing.

"Did you hear about what went down at the park yesterday?" Ashley interrupts the silence.

"No, what happened?" Craig looks up at her.

"There were some young guys in the park throwing rocks . . . at *old people* and *children*." Ashley puts her hand on her hip for effect.

"Wow, that's horrible. I hope no one was seriously injured."

"No, they were scared off before anyone was too hurt. It's like they have no good role models to look up to. I wonder if their parents know what they are doing." Ashley rolls her eyes.

51

"They need to focus more on their homework. I know I hardly have time to do anything besides school projects and work. It kind of sucks. But the semester will be over in a few months at least." Craig lets out a sigh.

Ashley laughs. "Maybe we can help distract you a little. Seems like you need it!"

"We could all go to dinner after work. I have some free time tonight." Craig sounds hopeful.

"I'm in!" Ashley says with almost too much enthusiasm.

"Great. It's a date." He pauses, then continues, "Yeah, I know I'll be even more free when the semester ends. I'll only have one more year, if things go as planned."

"You are so lucky you get to go to NYU!"

"I know. It's not that I'm not grateful I get to go. It's just so stressful sometimes, you know? Not just the workload but knowing my parents have high hopes of what I'll do with my degree when I finish. I don't even know if I'll continue to grad school."

"I'm sure you'll figure something out." Ashley tries to be encouraging.

"Yeah," Craig says before the room drops silent for a moment.

Craig hangs up his last bunch and comes over to me for another stack. I hand them to him. I am eavesdropping more than participating in the conversation. In general, I tend to observe from afar more than I participate, but for some reason I can't help but listen. A small part of me wishes I could be more involved.

"Have you seen the show called *Befriended* on Chillflix?" Craig asks me.

"Huh?" I look up at him, realizing he's talking to me.

"The show *Befriended*?"

"Oh, yeah. Just a few episodes," I stammer.

I talk to Craig for a few minutes about the show, and Ashley begins to interject her favorite moments of episodes I haven't seen yet. They talk about their favorite characters and jokes. I'm almost left out of the conversation again, not having seen

52

quite as many episodes as they have.

My mind begins to drift. Is there something between Ashley and Craig beyond friendship? She does seem a little immature for him, but he has a similar sense of humor. It may be Ashley has a flirtatious personality and the way she acts is natural to her. They seem like they've known each other for more than a few months. I don't know much about Craig outside of work. I haven't realized how much time he spends juggling work and school. I guess I haven't thought of him as the responsible type, more of a nerdy guy who likes making corny jokes. My mind wonders to what living with his roommates must be like, how many siblings he has if any, and what he wants to do after he gets out of school.

It is futile to think about these things. It only gives me a false hope for romance. I want to care, but people all disappear eventually. It usually takes a few years until I have to change my identity again, or else deal with the pain of outliving anyone I've gotten close to. Simple relationships are hard, and romantic ones have to be avoided entirely. I was once a married woman and will cherish those memories, but they can only be memories. Even with these reminders to myself, I can't stop entertaining the hope for a relationship in my life someday. Do I stand a chance of ever being happy in love again? Or should I just forget about it completely and move on?

As a girl I had many moments of uncertainty, but one of the biggest was when I was only seventeen, almost eighteen, years old. I was seated across the table from a man who was a few years older than I was. He had dark, warm eyes and thin lips. When he saw me look in his direction, he gave me a tentative smile.

We were seated with my parents and his parents, the Harts. This was not just any visit from family friends. I had to remind myself to breathe. In my mind I was scolding the maid who tightened my corset so even sitting was horribly uncomfortable.

My parents had given me a few clues to what this dinner was, but I read into it more than they had told me. The staff had prepared a special meal with expensive meats and had laid out the nicest of our family's silver and china. This made me nervous.

I knew my father was sick and would occasionally cough up blood. I noticed his moments of weakness and frailty. I was the last of four daughters to be married, and he wanted to make sure I was well off and secure before his passing. He knew I would not be looking for a higher level of class if I tried to find a husband for myself. I did not take finding a mate quite as seriously as my sisters did. There was a burning force of stubbornness in me from when I was born, as my mother always told me, but I would not let it interfere this time. I couldn't let my father get worse because of me.

I would just have to go along with it and hope for the best outcome. The Harts were family friends of my parents and lived nearby. I would occasionally see them at different local events my family was invited to, but I never really noticed or talked to any of their sons. Edmund was the son who was seated across from me, and this was our official introduction to one another. He was the most available of their sons and the closest to me in age.

After dinner our parents insisted Edmund and I go outside in the back for a short walk before we all joined each other for tea in the drawing room. We linked arms, and my dress shuffled every step that I took. My arm felt awkward and scrawny around his, and my gait quickened to keep up with his long strides. Even though we were outside, I knew privacy was only an illusion. Without a doubt our parents were spying and commenting about us through the windows as we went along.

During our first few meetings, we made polite small talk. Edmund was nice enough, even though we were still close to being strangers. At night, however, with an uncertain future in front of me, I had trouble sleeping. All my freedoms in my house with my family would be stripped away. I would be given away to a person I hardly knew and have the burden of managing a house, and those tending to it, by myself. How could my parents do this to me? Why couldn't I be trusted to find someone in my own time? I wasn't ready. It was coming too fast. I didn't feel up to the task but could not say anything.

11

Squealing pierces the air. I look up from my pile of clothes. Ashley is trying to grab a piece of jewelry from Carmen, but Carmen keeps bobbing up, down, and around the clothing racks, covering the perimeter of the store. Carmen must have pulled the plastic beads from the inventory pile out on the front counter. Ashley gives Carmen a fierce glare and crosses her arms. Craig and I pause our tasks, unsure how to help.

"Give it back NOW!" Ashley stomps her foot in frustration.

"But Stacy won't be dressed up enough for the party! She needs it!"

"Put it back or else I'm not letting you watch your show tomorrow," Ashley threatens. Carmen crinkles her face and shows a pouty lower lip.

"Fine!" Carmen throws the beads across the room, onto the counter, spilling several necklaces, earrings, and bracelets to the floor. Ashley eventually convinces her to pick them up.

I start to collapse the empty boxes and pile them on top of each other. Craig finishes hanging up the last of the clothing while Ashley hangs the necklaces on a small turning stand on the counter. Ashley was supposed to leave in the afternoon but was approved overtime for the amount of inventory that needed to be put away. It's almost closing time, and it's a relief we've been able to get the store back in order. Luckily, we've only had a few customers today.

Craig asks us if we are still interested in going out to dinner tonight. He suggests we eat at this great restaurant he discovered in Chinatown. We will have to take the bus, but Craig assures us it will be worth it. After all, there are a few more hours of sunlight left. Despite Carmen being a pain for Ashley, Ashley decides they should still go. Carmen has started to simmer down. I have nothing better to do, so I say I will go too. We put everything away and lock up before following Craig. About thirty minutes later, Craig pushes open the glass door of the restaurant and holds it open for us. I haven't been to a Chinese restaurant in a while, opting instead to heat up all my meals at home, although I do order Chinese delivery. A lady at the front guides us to two square tables put together, each covered with a white tablecloth. I sit across from Carmen, and the swinging of her legs shakes the whole table. Ashley, sitting next to her, puts a hand on her leg, signaling her to be still. We are handed plastic menus.

I have a moment to breathe. The room is small but more cozy than cramped. It is softly lit with a few sconces and a few hanging lights from the ceiling. The restaurant has a warm glow, contrasting the night sky outside with its deep shades of blue. The walls swim with illustrations of blue, orange, and red koi fish looping around each other against a background of bamboo shoots. Near the back of the restaurant stands a counter in front of the "To-Go" window, and on the counter sits a register next to a tip jar displaying a picture of a lucky cat with its paw up. There is a man behind the counter, and I hear a few cooks out of sight. A couple on the other side of the room lean over and whisper to each other. I order some dumplings, and Craig and Ashley both order the hand-pulled noodles. We return our menus to the server.

"It's a small place," Craig says, "but I'm sure you will thank me after you've tasted your food!"

"I bet," Ashley says while I nod in agreement.

"I have this paper coming up, which I should be writing now, but whatever, it can wait a few more hours. It's not the papers that are so bad. My business teacher, I can't wait to be done with him."

"Why is that?" I ask.

"He's so boring! He may know a lot of stuff, but man, can't he say it in a way that doesn't put the whole classroom to sleep? I have to sit in the front to force myself to stay awake. His voice has no energy to it," Craig vents.

"Like a robot or something?" Ashley laughs and then makes robotic beeping noises.

"Yeah!" Craig arches his eyebrows, and I grin at them.

Craig continues to go on about what he wants to do when he gets out of school for the summer. He wants to take what he calls a staycation, where it would be more affordable than going away. He also talks about seeing his family more and going to the beach with them. Carmen brightens up when he says "beach," and Ashley reassures her they will have plenty of beach trips over the summer. I secretly hope he invites me to come along.

Our server sets down our plates and bowls in front of us. I bend over my plate, and the steam rises in front of my face. The savory smells of our dishes make my mouth water. I take a bite of the dumpling I am holding with my chopsticks and look over to Ashley who is putting some of the noodles on a plate for Carmen. Ashley asks the server for a fork for Carmen. Craig is hunching over his bowl slurping up his noodles in large mouthfuls. After finishing one of my dumplings, I pour myself some of the green tea we ordered. I hear the front doorbell behind me ring.

There is a grungy-looking man who walks through the door and up to the counter. He has a baseball cap over his greasy hair, which is spilling down to his shoulders and covering part of his face. He is wearing an open flannel shirt with rolled-up sleeves over a white undershirt. The man appears sweaty and dirty even from a distance. He rings the bell on the counter and takes out his wallet as the restaurant owner makes his way to the register. The man gives the name for the to-go order he placed online, then places a twenty on the counter. The owner takes the bill and opens the register. I hear the click of something in the man's hand. The chattering of the couple on the other side of the room goes silent. Ashley sees the panic on my face.

"What's wrong?" Ashley asks before turning to look, and swears under her breath.

"Put it in there—now!" The man keeps his gun extended at the owner's chest while he throws him a plastic bag. The owner puts the bills from his register into the bag with trembling hands.

"Here." He hands the gunman the bag with his other arm raised.

"I know there's more," the man says with a snarl. "Give it to me!"

"That's all there is, I swear!"

The cashier keeps his hands raised and looks over to the seated couple. I can tell by the way the woman is crouched down and whispering into her phone, she is calling the police. The gunman picks up on it and flashes a glance in her direction. The owner tries to take advantage of the distraction and pushes the arm holding the gun down. He attempts to get the gun out of the man's hand. The bullets fire with loud cracks. The owner crumbles to the floor like a child's toy. The server comes toward the counter from the back, confused. She lets out a scream, and before she can run, she, too, is sent to the floor as bullets ring out. We can hear employees in the back heading toward the exit.

The gunman wastes no time. He fumbles with the owner on the ground trying to unhook the key ring from his belt. He tries several keys on the lockbox below the register before finding the right one, then fills his bag with more money.

We all look at each other and then back to the gunman, stunned and unsure what to do. My heart beats fast as I struggle to keep my breathing even. The legs of my chair make a squeaking noise as I push it out and stand beside it. I hope I am not too late. I quietly recite the phrase I was given by the messenger and begin to float upward.

The world becomes clear and crisp with all uncertainties falling from view. The cursed spirit is bound around the gunman's head and neck. Seeing me, it hisses loudly and constricts more tightly around the man.

I yell out, "In the name of the Mighty One, you will leave this place and enter the Forlorn!"

The inky legs of the cursed spirit melt off the man, and the orb at the center of its body fades away. Other close tempters and tormentors also evaporate. I allow myself to become heavy and drop back into my body. I am exhausted and have to lean against the back of the chair to hold myself up. The man looks around in a daze and drops the bag the instant he sees it. He starts crying when he looks down at the bodies on the floor and the blood spattered on his clothes. The man dodges glances with us as he stumbles toward the door. He disappears into the night. The woman from the couple sitting near us is bent over on her knees with her face glowing.

Ashley hugs Carmen close, trying to comfort her without knowing what to say. Carmen begins to cry in Ashley's arms. Ashley gently pries Carmen out of her arms so she can get a closer look at the crime scene. She walks away from Carmen at the table and peeks over the front counter. She grimaces and puts her hand over her mouth. I follow her while Craig watches Carmen at the table. The owner and the server are splayed out on the floor lying in dark puddles. Ashley wipes away a tear from her own cheek. I try to help her navigate her way to their bodies without getting any blood on her shoes. I speak quietly enough so Craig and Carmen won't hear. She squats down to each of them and places her hands over their bullet wounds. A few moments later she stands and holds out two bullets, then places them in my hand.

Craig now leaves Carmen at the table and meets us at the counter, looking confused. His eyes widen when he sees the owner and the server soaked in their own blood. The owner sits up and lets out a moan as he rubs his forehead.

"It's time to go," Ashley says with a little too much urgency.

I nod, understanding she would not have a good explanation for the owner or the server once they become clearheaded. Also, with a shooting there will be more questions from the police than the other crimes. I hear some sirens in the distance.

"Wait . . . shouldn't we wait around for . . . ," Craig asks, his voice trailing off. Ashley scoops up Carmen, and I follow them toward the door.

Ashley doesn't turn back to respond. I hear Craig's long strides trying to catch up behind us after we exit the restaurant. We all walk a few blocks in a hurry, then slow down a bit as we get closer to the bus stop. There are a few streetlights illuminating the sidewalk under the dark sky, but I still almost trip a few times.

"What happened? I don't get it." Craig waits for us to answer, but Ashley and I take quick glances at each other, keeping our eyes focused away from Craig. Craig is someone new I must decide whether or not to trust. Can we let anyone else know about this spirit world? What will Craig do if we tell him? I sit with Ashley and Carmen on the bus stop bench. Craig fidgets and paces in silence until our bus arrives.

12

I shake out my umbrella before I enter the café. I wipe my boots off on the rug inside the door. The dim afternoon light shines through the large front windows, filtering through the heavy clouds. There are different groupings of small tables on the left side of the room. The walls are white with colorful but generic paintings of potted plants and loaves of bread. On the right is a pastry case behind which a woman in an apron stands and takes orders. The signs on the wall behind the counter are giant chalkboards displaying the barely legible menu.

Students and older couples are bending over their meals of soups and sandwiches, deep in conversation. It takes me a minute for me to see Craig near the back. As I pass the tables, I hear the light tones of dialogue in the background and the clinking of kitchen tools coming from the kitchen. Craig is typing away at his computer, not noticing me until I sit at his table. He looks up and closes his laptop. Craig asks if I want something to eat. He lists off a few choices from the menu from memory, and I pick the cranberry chicken sandwich. I remain at the table as he goes up to order for us. I usually refuse if people offer to buy food for me, but this time I don't. I feel as if I am burdening them if I accept, but with Craig is seems like it would be a burden if I refuse.

I worked with Craig Monday morning, two days ago, and he texted me after our shift about wanting to meet up to talk about something. I'm guessing it has something to do with what happened on Sunday at the restaurant. When I worked with him on Monday, he probably noticed I avoided talking to him besides what was necessary for work. Craig's text sounded serious, though, so I agreed. Is there something else he wants to discuss but can't at work? I shift in my chair while watching two college-aged girls laugh about something on one of their phones. I look down at my hands and start to pick away at the cuticles. Craig comes back to the table and tucks his laptop away into his backpack hanging from the back of his chair.

"I'm trying to finish a paper that's due today. It's the one I told you about, for my finance class. But hey, it's better than my usual 'start it the day it's due,' 'load up on caffeine because I only had three hours of sleep' routine."

"Wow." I give him a bemused look.

"Well, it is an improvement, you have to give me that." Craig points his finger at me jokingly.

"Yeah, true."

"Oh yeah, I wanted to show you the app I just released." Craig hands me his phone with the app opened.

I follow the directions on the screen. It's one of those puzzle games where you have to line up the shapes in the correct order to beat the level. Each level takes a little bit longer than the last.

"Pretty cool, huh?" he asks, and I nod while looking down at the screen. "Better than business stuff at least. I made that app along with a few others. I really wish I could do something like it after I graduate and still find a way to pay for everything. Our professors don't really teach us small business stuff, you know?"

"Yeah, I can imagine they would want you to work at one of the big businesses in the city."

"I could do something like start my own business, but it would be really tough. Maybe I could work my way up to it. I have all these ideas I want to try out. I want to do something

63

really cool. Like what if you could order a pizza, but instead of a delivery guy bringing it to you, a drone drops it off at your doorstep. You wouldn't even have to pay a tip!"

The corners of my mouth spread into a smile.

"Just imagine if you could order pizza and like that"—he snaps his fingers—"it lands right on your stoop." His hand mimics the drone flying and landing as he makes a sound effect for its motor.

I laugh at his wild, wide-eyed expressions and gestures. He has a sparkle in his eyes and a contagious enthusiasm. In a few moments we are both bent over laughing, passing ideas back and forth of what app-controlled drones could do. Who needs to walk their dog when a drone can do it? Why drive to work when a drone could carry you there? The buzzer on our table goes off, and Craig gets our food from the counter.

Craig places my cranberry chicken sandwich in front of me and sits down with his sandwich. I wait for Craig to start eating before taking a large bite out of one of my sandwich halves. I listen to those talking around us as we enjoy our own food.

After a few minutes I tell Craig, "Thank you for lunch."

"It's no problem." Craig finishes chewing his mouthful and looks up at me. "I bet you're wondering why I wanted you to come," Craig says.

I put my sandwich down and wipe my hands on my napkin.

"Have you seen Ashley at work this week?" Craig asks.

"Yeah, I worked with her yesterday. Why?"

"Well, I asked her about what happened on Sunday and she wouldn't tell me. She just said she didn't want to talk about it. I was hoping you would."

"What do you mean? Tell you what?" I ask him.

"It just seemed a little weird."

"Oh, so you don't normally see people getting shot?" I answer sarcastically.

"No, it's *how* it happened."

I take a sip of my water, waiting for him to continue.

"I could see the man was taking all the money from the lockbox behind the counter . . . But then he just froze and looked like he didn't know where he was. He started crying out of nowhere and left. He left without the money. I don't get it."

"Maybe he changed his mind?" I say, sounding ridiculous.

"I also remember you standing up and saying something weird right before he seemed to break down."

I start to pick at my cuticles again.

"Then there was what Ashley did. She not only looked at the bodies but crouched beside them. She handed you something she found. The one guy who was shot sat up. You both were also very eager to leave before the police arrived."

"I . . . I don't know what to say." I can't bring myself to lie to Craig, but I can't tell him the complete truth either. He can see it on my face.

There are a few minutes of us looking at the remaining pieces of our sandwiches. I notice a few customers coming and going and the people ordering their food. I look down at the scuff marks on my boots and play with the zipper on my jacket.

Craig finally breaks the silence. "This may sound crazy, but I had an idea of what was going to happen in the restaurant."

I stop fidgeting and look at him in confusion.

"I had a dream something terrible was going to happen. I knew but couldn't keep away. I felt pulled toward it. I had a feeling you and Ashley needed to be there to fix it. I wasn't sure how. I have had these dreams for many years but a lot of times can't do anything about them. I have been having a lot of strange dreams lately, in fact. I remember when you and Ashley told me about the kids throwing rocks in the park. I had a dream about that a few nights before. Sometimes my dreams are good ones, or at least they don't turn out as bad as I think they will, but I had a strong feeling about the one at the restaurant."

"So, you took us to a place knowing we would be in danger?" I felt my temper rising a little.

"My dreams are a little blurry at times, but in this one it looked like neither of you would get hurt. It has been so frustrating to have these dreams but no ability to do anything about them. Sure, sometimes I try to intervene, but most times

65

it's too much for me to do anything. I knew somehow that you and Ashley could save the people there."

My anger fizzles out, and I become more intrigued than anything. Craig looks into the distance.

"I also met a man in this café. He told me you and Ashley needed me and not to ignore my dreams when I have them. He knew my name and a lot of things I have never told anyone. It was very strange. He called himself—"

"The messenger?" I interrupt.

Craig looks shocked. "You've met this guy already?"

I take the two bullets out of my jacket pocket left there from the other night, and I place them into Craig's hand. They still have flecks of blood on them. He turns one over in his hand, studying it. What are the chances another coworker of mine also has an extraordinary ability? The messenger must have come to him for a reason. It must be part of some bigger plan.

"Ashley . . . she was able to heal the people who were shot. She even took the bullets right out of them. She healed me once too."

Craig places the bullets down on his napkin, then moves to the edge of his seat waiting for me to continue.

"Ashley and I have both seen the messenger. He gave me phrases when I first met him. The first one brings me to this place where I can see the dark and light spirits influencing people. The other one allows me to get rid of the dark ones."

"What do these dark spirits do to people?"

I tell him more about the tormentors and tempters in the spirit world. I give him a brief overview of the woman on the fire escape, the teenagers in the park, and how the jazz man choked me and was following me.

"The more tormentors and tempters we can get rid of, the greater chance people have to be free. Also, we can only take down Levizar after getting rid of his followers." I study his face. His eyes are wide in amazement.

"Wow, that makes way more sense. I knew there was something else you weren't telling me! I never thought there were other people out there similar to me." Craig gives me a "told you so" smile.

"The messenger told me those who have these abilities have had their hearts tested and have passed. Do you ever remember a moment of some sort of testing? Both Ashley and I can't remember ours."

"Hmm, I don't think so."

Craig and I continue to talk about the spirit world and about how his dreams have lined up with the things I have seen in Manhattan. I sit back in my chair, relieved we can talk openly about it. I trust him more now, knowing about his dreams and how the messenger came to him.

I am glad I can talk to Ashley and Craig about the job the messenger has lined up for me. I don't have to bear my struggles alone. However, I also know there is another side of myself they can never know. How many years will it take for them to notice I don't age? Or when will they notice my background story is a lie? I push down these anxious thoughts for a few more minutes as Craig begins to joke about what our undercover hero names would be if we had to choose. The more time I get to spend with Craig, the more I enjoy his company. His jokes are foolish, but I cannot help but laugh.

A few weeks had passed since I had been introduced to Edmund. On a few occasions he came over with his family and we would walk out into the back after we ate. A few days ago, he sent a letter saying he would come with his coachman and, if I was available, take me in his carriage to town. I sent him a letter saying I would be waiting for his arrival. I waited near the front windows by the door. So far we had only had light conversation involving mundane topics such as the weather, gardening, and music.

I said my good-byes to my family as I noticed his carriage approaching. I was helped into the carriage by Edmund, and we were on our way down the road.

"How are you today, Eliza?"

"I am doing well. How about yourself?" I asked in return.

"I could not get much sleep last night. Other than being tired, I am well."

The conversation dropped after these obligatory greetings. I did not mind, but stared out the window at the trees flanking the road and the flowers. I could hear Edmund shifting in his seat next to me, not as comfortable with the silence. After a few minutes I could see the town in the distance.

Once we arrived, Edmund helped me down from the carriage, and we started to walk along the shop fronts down the cobblestone street. He put his arm out, and I linked my arm with his. We each peered into different windows as we walked. The light conversation was like a vapor, similar to the others we had had in the past. Edmund insisted on talking on and on about the weather. Would the clouds continue to come in? If they did, would it rain? If it rained, would there be flooding? He smiled in my direction every few minutes, and I smiled back. Inside I suffered. If he didn't start another topic soon, I might scream.

I told him I thought my father was sick. Edmund looked down at me, into my eyes, and asked me how sick I thought he was. I told him I wasn't sure but had a feeling it was bad. Both of us were silent for a moment, and then he told me he was sorry and hoped his health would improve. We continued to admire items in the windows, but otherwise, we had little conversation. I thought it was perhaps better than discussing irrelevant topics like the weather.

We walked into one shop where necklaces were aligned in a glass case. There was one I couldn't help but admire. It had a small red ruby in the center. I must have said I liked it without realizing it because before I knew it, Edmund purchased it and clasped it around my neck. I blushed. I couldn't help but be flattered but was also embarrassed he went through the trouble of buying it.

Edmund and I continued our walk down the street. He let out a big yawn, like the many he had made today.

"Am I boring you?" I asked, finding it difficult to hide my aggravation. "Do you have any real interest in me at all?"

To my surprise Edmund turned to me and held both of my gloved hands out in between us. He had a serious expression on his face.

"Eliza, I was yawning not because of boredom but because I could not sleep last night. How could I? I was up all night thinking about how not to make a fool out of myself with you. I hold your impressions in high esteem. I know you are not a girl who is easily swayed by things most would be. Most men would find independent thought to be intimidating, but I admire it. I can also say the compassion you have for your family is endearing. Please amuse me a while longer before you dismiss me."

I nodded and put my head down in shame. I thought he saw our relationship as an obligation and not something to be cultivated. It had not occurred to me that he could be in search of more than what was expected of him by his family. My fingers stroked the pendant on the necklace he had given me.

13

I take a few items of clothing off the go-back rack. It's not hard to find where they belong in the store. The familiar shoulder-padded suit jackets and chevron-patterned skirts are the same ones that always end up on the go-back rack. My guess is they were not sewn to fit how they should or they look better on the hanger than once customers try them on. I'm not even sure why people would try them on in the first place. There are few items in the store I would take even if someone gave them to me for free.

Mr. Hardy is at the front desk looking over some paperwork, with his glasses on the tip of his nose and a pen in his hand. He has been pretty quiet the whole morning except for him greeting us at the beginning of our shift. I look over to one of my coworkers, Tina, who is bringing back some hangers from the fitting room. You would think our customers would be decent enough to hang the clothing back on the hangers. Retail has a way of revealing the lazy side of people.

I grab another stack of clothing from the rack to put away and Tina joins me. We don't talk much, each lost in our own thoughts. I am glad I was able to meet up with Craig at the café yesterday, and I appreciate his willingness to tell me about his dreams. It sounds like they have been a burden on him for many years. I hope he realizes I am still only one person and also have my limitations. I probably won't be able to fix every bad thing from his nightmares. Craig's eyes tend to have a sparkle in them when he laughs; his whole face lights up. His laugh is infectious. I haven't laughed that loud in a while. I smile to myself. A coldness in me seems to melt away whenever we talk to each other. Just being in his presence makes me lighter, but I also know it is dangerous to daydream about anything coming from it.

Tina and I greet a few customers who come in over the few hours of our shift. Some need help finding something specific, while most are just browsing. Tina talks about her two kids and the different activities they are in and how they are doing in school. Whenever she asks me questions, I give vague answers and lead with another question about herself or her family. I shy away from giving away too many details about my created identity so I won't raise any questions later if I can't remember what I've said. My phone vibrates. I walk behind a row of round racks so Mr. Hardy doesn't see me take it out of my pocket.

"You want to come over today?" The text is from Ashley.

"Sure, I'm off in an hour," I text back.

Is there something she needs? I haven't been invited over besides the day the jazz man attacked me at work. I don't bother texting to ask but figure I will talk to her when we see each other. Tucking my phone back into my pocket, I walk around the store seeing if there is anything I can put back into place. Maybe Ashley just needs some company. She told me she has today off.

I knock on Ashley's door. I shake out my umbrella. It started raining a lot on my way over, though it's only a few blocks away. Even though the temperatures have been higher, the rain still makes my hands cold. Hopefully in the next few weeks the rain will stop altogether.

I am glad there was no drama at work and I only had to work until the afternoon. All our customers today tended to be pretty levelheaded, their requests not too outlandish. Some ladies tend to complain about the prices, and I have to remind them I only work there, I don't set the prices.

"Hey," Ashley says as she opens the door. I walk inside.

Their apartment is less cluttered than when I was there last. There are still coloring books and dolls, but they have been set neatly on the table. I assume Ashley put the dirty dishes in the sink before I came. Ashley's fashion rack has had some additions, with new outfits I haven't seen yet.

"Having a good day off so far?" I ask Ashley.

"Yeah, I finished sewing this skirt for an outfit I've been putting together." She holds up a black high-waisted pleated skirt with a thin belt through the loopholes.

"Cute." I run my hand across the skirt as she holds it out for me to look at it.

"How was work?"

"It was fine. Nothing exciting."

I sit on her couch, and she asks if I want any coffee. I can't refuse free coffee, so I say yes. She goes to start a pot of coffee while I sit in silence. Ashley puts some sugar packets on the table, along with creamer and two mugs for us both. She joins me on the couch while we wait for the coffee to brew. The enticing smell of the beans starts to make its way into the living room.

Ashley hands me a sketch of the next outfit she plans to sew for the fashion competition. She explains you have to make several outfits all coinciding with one theme that tell something about yourself as a designer. I'm impressed at her different ideas, especially since she hasn't been designing for very many years. I find it humorous how stark a contrast today's fashion is to what I would have worn in Victorian years in England. In some of my old outfits, I had trouble sitting comfortably or walking briskly without becoming out of breath.

Ashley puts away her sketchbook and pours us our mugs of coffee. I go over to the table to add my regular amount of sugar and creamer. The steam rises into my face as I hold my mug close and take small sips, careful not to burn the roof of my mouth. She puts away the sugar and creamer, and we bring our coffee to drink on the couch. I sit with my legs crossed under me, getting comfortable.

"That was crazy what happened the other day at the restaurant," Ashley starts.

"Yeah." I nod in agreement.

"I mean, I have met some creeps, but I've never actually seen a shooting. Those poor people."

I listen, drinking my coffee.

"I can't stop thinking about the way they fell to the floor like that. One minute they were fine and the next they were bleeding all over. I bet they were really scared. They probably thought they wouldn't make it. I wonder what they told their families about it."

"If it weren't for you, they wouldn't be with their families now."

"Yeah," Ashley says with a half smile, "I keep thinking about what could have happened, though. I keep having nightmares of them screaming out for me to save them . . . but I can't . . . I don't reach them in time." A tear runs down the side of Ashley's face.

"Craig told me he has dreams . . . but not normal dreams. Dreams about things that are going to happen. I bet he feels the same way."

"Dreams of the future?"

"Yeah, and it sounds as if he has had them for a while."

"Was there a specific dream he told you about?" Ashley asks.

"Craig said he had a dream about what would happen at the Chinese place. He wasn't sure what would happen, but he thought we could do something . . . And you did. You saved two people."

"He put us in danger without letting us know first?"

"Yeah, but—"

"That's not okay. What if something had happened to Carmen? I would feel responsible."

"He wasn't sure—"

"It doesn't matter if he was sure or not. If he told me, I

73

would have at least left Carmen at home."

I nod, and the room goes quiet. I place my mug down on the coffee table. Ashley apologizes and says she shouldn't yell at me because it's not my fault. I worry she is going to place all the blame on Craig. Craig meant well, but at the same time good intentions don't always give good results. I probably should have waited for Craig to tell her about his dreams, but I somehow felt it was important she knows about it. After all, there has to be some sort of purpose behind what the messenger has told us. Maybe we are meant to work together. The messenger said to keep close to those in my circle, but I hope telling Ashley about Craig's dreams doesn't cause a rift among us. I can only hope for the best.

14

I run my fingers down the dresses on one of the round racks. I find one not with its own style. I take it out and look around for its correct place. As I place the dress on the correct rack, Ashley is sitting on the stool behind the front desk, reading her magazine. Every few minutes, amidst chomping her gum, she chuckles at what she reads. Craig is a few feet away from me, also looking for misplaced items on the sales floor. He lowers his face into his hands and rubs his face.

"Are you okay?" I ask him.

"Yeah, I'm okay. I'm just super tired from staying up late to finish my papers and studying. It's probably my fault for not planning ahead. I should have started studying sooner." He gives me a weak smile, but I can tell something else is bothering him.

"How did your paper turn out?"

"Boring. Very dry. But at the same time, I think it's close to what he is looking for."

"Good."

"I'm going to get some coffee from the back." Craig points toward the employee area.

"That coffee? I think it's from this morning."

"So?"

"It's a few hours old and probably doesn't taste great." My sour expression makes Craig laugh.

"For sure. But I'm too tired to care." He lifts his eyebrows up at me before turning to go to the back. My cheeks grow warm.

The afternoon lull passes after a few hours, and ladies who have just gotten off work are coming into Sheila's Boutique. I ask a few customers if I can help them find anything, but they all tell me they are fine, just looking. Craig gets one lady who says he looks like the spitting image of her grandson, and grabs his cheek. Ashley looks up from her magazine with a wide grin as Craig pulls himself away.

After the old lady leaves, Ashley explodes with laughter, bent over the counter. Her laugh makes me laugh, so I, too, am bent over one of the racks, almost unable to catch my breath. We continue to laugh while Craig stands there sheepish, wiping his glasses on his shirt. He doesn't laugh.

"Come on, guys. It wasn't *that* funny." Craig glares at us.

"Oh, really? I'm surprised she didn't give you a kiss!" Ashley taunts.

Craig lets out a sigh.

Ashley and I finally quiet down, and she pulls out her magazine from behind the counter.

"Did anyone want to go for some pizza after work?" Craig asks, changing the topic.

"Sure," I say, trying not to sound too eager.

"There isn't going to be any gunman there too, is there?" Ashley looks up with a glare from her magazine.

"What do you—" Craig begins.

"You know exactly what I'm talking about. You knew people were going to get hurt but let me bring my little sister anyway."

"How did you—"

"I'm sorry, I told her about your dreams," I tell Craig. He looks surprised.

"So . . . no, I'm not going. I don't think I can trust you yet. And I do have to watch Carmen again." Ashley looks back

76

down at her magazine and flips the page with more force than needed.

"I'm sorry," Craig says, "I'll tell you not to bring Carmen next time."

"I can still go," I say trying to cheer him up. He gives me a half smile and nods.

The rest of our shift continues in almost complete silence. The only words we share with each other are related to doing our jobs. I put away a few items from the go-back rack with Craig while Ashley wipes down the counter and organizes it. At the end of our shift, we grab our bags from our lockers. We file out and Ashley locks the door behind us. We all say our good nights; then Ashley heads home while I am left with Craig to find dinner.

The streetlights turn on altogether once the night has drawn closer. Craig is kicking some rocks on the sidewalk with his hands in his pockets. He has not said very much the few blocks we have walked together. Something besides the lack of sleep must be getting to him. We have a block or two left until we reach the pizza place. A few people have passed us who are probably looking for a place to eat too.

"Is something wrong?" I ask Craig.

"Not really." He looks up at me and then back down to the sidewalk.

"If it was the lady at the shop . . ."

"No, it wasn't anything you guys did," Craig says.

"Are you upset I told Ashley about your dreams?" I prod.

Craig shakes his head. "I don't care you told her."

I wait a moment, not wanting to press him too much on it.

"Over spring break, I went to China with my business class. They talked about innovation, getting ahead and stuff like that. When I came back, my parents asked me when I planned to start applying for grad school. I kept telling them I was thinking about it, trying to get things lined up. Really, I was just stalling. When I told them I wasn't interested in going to school after undergrad, they freaked out."

"Oh, I'm sorry."

"I am paying for a part of my school, but since they're helping pay for a lot of it, they feel like they have a say in what I do with my future. I'm grateful I get to go, but what if I don't want to work at the kind of job they want me to? I know I don't want to. Why would I continue school when I could be looking for the experience I need?" Craig pauses a moment. "It's just a mess."

"That's a lot of pressure."

"Yeah, tell me about it." I can imagine him rolling his eyes behind his glasses.

A part of me lightens up. I'm glad I didn't say something to upset him. I wish I could stop myself from caring so much, but instead, I want to put my arm around him and tell him things with his parents will be okay. I want to ask him if there is something I can do to help. Saying these things would only make me more attached. We continue down the street, and I refrain from saying anything else.

I see the pizza sign lit up in the distance. We hear a woman's scream. A short man in baggy sweat pants and a dark blue hoodie is aiming his gun at a woman who looks like she just got into her car a half block ahead of us. The man has wedged himself between the car door and the woman. The young woman looks down, raising her acrylic-nailed hands in surrender. A jolt of fear sweeps through me, and my feet are glued to the pavement.

"Get out!" the gunman yells.

He jabs her with the end of his gun, and she slides out onto the ground. With his free hand, he grabs her arm and drags her aside so he can slide into her sedan. He closes the door and starts the engine with the keys she had left in the ignition. The man has to drive back and forth a couple times to exit the tight parallel space where it was parked. He taps the cars in front and behind several times.

I mutter the phrase "Open my eyes and allow me to see the truth behind the inner movements of every life."

I rise up into the spirit world embracing the same awe and wonder as I do each time I enter it. A tempter is choking the car thief, probably telling the man he needed more thrill in his life; he needed to take a risk. If he wanted it, he could reach out and take it. The spirit lets out a shrill laugh in my direction. Goose bumps speckle my arms on my body below. The man is able to pull the car out, and the car starts to speed away.

I yell out the second phrase before he gets any further. I watch the cursed spirit yell out and melt away. I let out a sigh of relief as I let myself sink back into my body. If I had waited a few seconds later, he might having gotten too far out of my reach. The car swerves but then stops. The man inside looks around, confused. He puts the car in park and hops out, slamming the door behind him, and takes off. The car is left idling in the middle of the road.

I grab Craig's arm, almost losing my balance.

"Woah, you okay?" he asks, supporting me with the crook of his arm.

"Yeah . . . I just need to sit down."

I sit on the bus stop bench as Craig checks on the woman. She is standing with her arms tight around herself.

"Are you hurt?" Craig asks her.

"I'm only scraped up a little," the woman replies, giving him a faint smile with her red lips. The driver in the car behind hers lays on the horn. Craig calls the police for her, and she reparks her car while waiting for them to show up.

After a few minutes, a police officer shows up and asks for the young woman's statement. He asks how injured she is, and she says she's fine. We give as many details of the gunman as we can from what we remember. Once the officer is gone, the woman thanks us, locks her car door behind her, and drives away.

I stand up from the bench, almost losing my balance again. Craig grabs my arm to help me steady myself. I try to convince him I'm okay. We walk the remaining distance to the pizza restaurant.

I take eager bites of my pizza as I observe the other customers. I can overhear some of them talking about the man with the gun who was outside a while ago. Others are oblivious, chatting about their coworkers and other trivial complaints. There are also some students talking about what tests they bombed recently.

"It would have been nice if Ashley came with us," Craig states.

"Yeah," I say, a bit guilty that I feel glad we get to spend more time together without her.

"The lady was probably okay, but she may have been more hurt than she admitted."

"Wait! Is this something you saw in one of your dreams?"

Craig goes quiet, taking another big bite of his pizza.

"Is this the only reason you asked us to come?" Does he just want to use us? Or does he really want to spend time with us . . . with me? Maybe he only needs me to get rid of the dark spirits.

"No . . . I mean, I do like hanging out with you guys too. I was going to say something, but Ashley seemed so upset. Do you think Ashley would have come if I'd told her about my dream? Especially after being so mad at me for the last one?" Craig asks almost in a rhetorical way.

"Probably not." I slump back on my side of the booth.

"It may seem as if I'm not being honest—"

"Oh, really? How could I ever think that?" I say with sarcasm.

"Like I was telling you before, I have had these dreams for a while now," Craig continues unfazed. "Ever since high school. And I felt this urgency to go find out when and where these things would happen. Sometimes it was fuzzy, and other times I could figure it out. A lot of times I would go and see these bad things happen over and over, and I had to sit back and watch them happen. There was nothing I could do about them. If what the messenger told me was true, there is something now we can do. I heard you mumbling some strange words, then the carjacker decides he is no longer interested in the car and leaves. When your eyes were no longer glazed over, you almost fell to the ground. I could see how drained you looked."

80

"After the cursed spirit left the man, he could see what it was he was doing," I explain.

Craig gives me a wide smile and then continues eating his pizza.

I smile back, unable to be angry at him. "Maybe just give me a heads-up next time?

"Sure thing."

After a month of dating, Edmund had invited me to a picnic on his parents' property. We sat together on a blanket with a heavy wicker basket placed in between us. The dappled light glistened above us, and the sun made the small lake sparkle. A mother duck waddled past us with her ducklings following close behind her. One by one, the ducklings bobbed up and down beneath the water's surface, plunging into the water after their mother. I picked a few pink wildflowers poking up from beneath the edges of the blanket. Edmund took off his hat and asked if I was ready to eat. I nodded.

I ran my fingers over the small ruby in the necklace Edmund had given me a week earlier. It was embarrassing that I had lashed out at him when we were in town. I had thought I was boring him and he wanted to leave as soon as he could. In my mind it was only an obligation to him to see I was taken care of. I thought it was something he had promised my father and nothing else. I was flattered he cared about my opinion but also afraid I had ruined any good impression he might have had.

"I really appreciate the necklace you gave me. It is beautiful."

"The pleasure is mine," Edmund said as he started taking out food from the basket.

Edmund pulled out roast beef sandwiches with cheese and lettuce, a pigeon pie, sardines with crackers, and fresh strawberries. I was overwhelmed at the amount of choices he brought, seeing the basket still had more food. He said he wanted to give me options, not certain yet of what food I liked. Edmund handed me some lemonade. I thanked him as I tried to decide what I wanted to start with first. I picked up a sandwich and started taking small bites as we both dodged small, awkward glances at each other. Would I be able to keep myself from saying something stupid this time? Was he hurt from what I had said before?

"You said you wanted to read some of my poetry?" I began.

"Yes, I'm curious about what you write," Edmund said after swallowing his food.

I took a small, folded-up piece of paper out of my pocket. I unfolded it and handed it to him. He began to read it as I took nervous bites out of my sandwich. His expression looked focused, but I could not get anything else from it. The poem was a few stanzas telling about a mystery but also an enjoyment and hope for the future. He began to smirk as he read. I had hoped he could tell I was more optimistic about our relationship than I had led him to believe before. Edmund told me he liked it, and I felt my uneasiness melt away.

Edmund and I talked more about other poems I had written and also books we had read. As we broke into the apple turnovers and cheesecake, we talked about our relationships with our siblings and about family members who were too busy interfering with others' lives rather than focusing on their own. I was getting really full and enjoyed the sun as we laughed, joined in deeper conversation than all our other times together.

15

A week has passed since we witnessed the attempted carjacking. Craig is helping Ashley carry some boxes of new clothing out from the back. He hands them to me, and I sort the boxes to make unpacking them easier for us. I avert my gaze from Craig, realizing I have been staring longer than intended. I take a box cutter from the counter and start opening them to make sure the items inside match the label on the outside of each box.

In the last several days, I had made a few trips to my favorite coffee shop but otherwise done little else. I was surprised to receive a text from Craig a few days ago. He told me about another dream he had, so we met each other by one of the student buildings. One man had a knife and was going around stabbing people. I was able to make the spirit leave him but not before he had attacked three people. I wished Ashley was there to help us. I texted her to see if she could meet us, but it took her a few hours to respond. When she did, she asked if I wanted to hang out. I said I'd had a question about something but ended up figuring it out. As far as I knew, no one died from any of their wounds. We were lucky.

A day later, there was a robbery Craig told me was going to happen. It was a liquor store with another gunman. I was relieved no bullets were fired. We were also successful on this task. I've been happy to get more chances to spend time with Craig and hope he also enjoys my company. I'm still not sure how he sees me, but either way, I am grateful for the time I do get with him.

Ashley starts assorting jewelry from one of the smaller boxes on the counter. Once we have unloaded one box, I hang up a few tops; then Craig finds places in the store to hang the remaining items while I start on the next box.

"Your sweater looks nice," Craig adds.

"Oh . . . thanks!" I blush and turn away to my work. Even after two hundred years, I still get embarrassed by compliments. I had bought a new fuzzy pink sweater to wear with my black jeans, changing it up from my usual graphic T-shirts. I felt foolish buying a new piece of clothing, one I wouldn't normally wear, just because I had hoped he would notice.

Ashley lets out a sound of disgust as she tries untangling the jewelry.

"Everything okay over there?" I ask her.

"This stupid jewelry is so ugly it's not even worth untangling. I should just throw it in the trash!" Ashley slams the necklace down on the counter. "I mean, how many people will buy it anyway? Mr. Hardy gets worse in his style awareness with every order he makes. It's like he's picking out what he wishes his ex would wear to scare off the other men. Who buys this stuff anyway, other than the pampered, beauty-salon, on-the-fifth-husband type?" Ashley fumes.

"Woah, that's a little harsh," I say, trying to suppress a laugh.

"Sorry, it's just . . . you know the fashion contest I told you I entered?"

"Yeah."

"I submitted my designs and I didn't get through the first round. And I hold this place responsible! How am I ever supposed to heighten my fashion sense being around this crap all day?" Ashley grabs a suit jacket with shoulder padding and a large mismatching sequin flower on the front, which I had just hung up, and shakes it in the air looking like she will scream.

I can't help laughing at her. "Well, it's a paycheck at least," I tell her.

"I guess you're right." Ashley sits behind the counter on her stool, attempting again to untangle the jumbled pile of necklaces.

"One day I'm sure you will enjoy telling people about your sad retail-day beginnings when you have made it," Craig adds, trying to cheer her up.

"Hopefully." Ashley lets out a sigh.

Soon we are able to get into a rhythm and have most of the boxes emptied. Helping Ashley, we get all the jewelry on its stands and organized on the counter. I take the box cutter and collapse the boxes and stack them in the back room. We encounter only a few customers during our entire shift.

Craig leans over to me. "I had another dream again. I think I know where we should go, but it would be after work. Are you in?"

"What are you mumbling about?" Ashley asks.

"Um . . ." Craig searches for an answer.

"You aren't referring to what's in your dreams again, are you? I heard you say *dream*."

"We have helped a few people," I start, when Craig doesn't say anything, "and I think you should join us."

"Why, so I can be shot?" Ashley rolls her eyes.

"No, so you can heal the injured people. They need you. The text I sent you the other day . . . people were hurt. They ended up being okay, but they might not have."

"Well, I told you I didn't want Carmen to be there, not that I wouldn't ever want to help."

"I had a dream about something happening tonight," Craig interjects. "Are you coming?"

"Maybe I do need a good distraction." Ashley smiles.

16

Over the past few weeks, Craig has been telling us more of his dreams. Most of them he is clear on where they are by locating different landmarks in his dreams, or he has a feeling of the area and takes a guess. Sometimes he tells us they are too blurry, and he admits he wishes he could do more. I always reassure him what he is trying to do is good enough. Ashley has been more cautious than we have, always asking a lot of questions, only a few of which Craig is able to answer. She still goes with us and helps anyone who ends up getting hurt.

We have seen a variety of crimes we were able to help stop. There was a lady who was cornered in an alley with two men waiting to take advantage of her. Another day a few pickpockets ended up dropping the wallets and valuables they had snatched. Some of them were able to return the items before being seen by their victims. There were two men fighting outside a bar who ended up apologizing to each other, forgetting what it was they were mad about in the first place. We stopped a teenage boy who smashed someone's car window and was about to drive off in the car.

We all decided to take today off from work. We've needed a break. We were able to request the day off from the boutique, and Craig is celebrating finishing his finals. I'm holding under my arm my large bag containing my towel, flip-flops, and sunscreen. I'm trying to remember the last time I wore shorts and a light hoodie instead of my usual thick jacket and dark jeans. The sunglasses I just bought a day earlier are resting on my face. Ashley is also holding her bag with her belongings, and Craig is content with holding his towel. Carmen is skipping alongside us, holding Ashley's hand.

A few minutes have passed since we entered the Coney Island amusement park. We are walking around, looking at everything before we decide what to do first. Craig keeps talking about how relieved he feels being done with all his finals and never having to see some of his professors again. It will still be a few days before he gets his grades back, but he's certain he did above average. But he still seems distracted and has been staring off into the distance more than usual.

"Is something wrong?" I ask him.

"I have been having that dream again." Craig looks down at the ground.

Craig told Ashley and me a week ago about a dream where people were being attacked in a subway station. He said in the dream there were guys dressed in black and many people on the ground in their blood. Every time he has this dream, their screams get louder, but unfortunately there is no landmark to identify the specific subway station. Ashley was concerned, but she said she would be willing to risk it for one day so Carmen can have her day at the beach. We promised we would tell her if anything looked out of place.

I look over at Ashley and Carmen who are farther ahead of us. "I'll make sure to tell everyone if I see anything strange," I reassure Craig.

"Thanks. That makes me feel a little better." He smiles at me, and we speed up our pace to match Ashley's and Carmen's strides.

Craig seems a little less distracted as he talks about his two older sisters; one lives in Jersey still, and the other moved to Ohio a few years ago. I struggle to hear him over the people screaming on the roller coaster. I hope we are able to notice any danger before it happens, although he hasn't mentioned something bad happening here. I look around at the colorful rides, noticing how different it looks from decades ago. I am amazed they have anything historical left of this park, but it's nice they were able to restore it. It looks as though school has ended for a lot of college students and children, and many are here with their families. One little girl is holding cotton candy the size of her head. Carmen points to it and begs Ashley if she can have some. Ashley tells her, "Maybe later."

"Ooh, I want to go on the Cyclone!" Craig says, pointing to the massive roller coaster.

"That looks fun! But I don't think Carmen is big enough to go on that ride." Ashley looks down at Carmen, who is looking at a rock she found.

"It's okay. I can watch her if you want," I offer.

"Really? Are you sure?"

I nod, and she tells me to make sure to hold her hand so she doesn't run off like she did the other day. I reach down and grab her little clammy hand into mine. Ashley and Craig go wait in a short line for the ride while Carmen looks up at me with widened eyes.

"How old are you?" Carmen studies my face.

"Um, how old do you think?"

"52?"

"No, that's not it." I suppress my laughter. She is closer than most people get. Carmen tells me she is nine in only three more months. I ask her a few more questions, and she tells me about being excited to start fourth grade because it's closer to being in fifth grade. Carmen mentions two friends she likes playing horsey with during recess. I point to a bracelet on her arm she is playing with, and ask her where it came from. Her smile widens, and she says she and Ashley made friendship bracelets two nights ago. Ashley once told me they didn't have a father, that he was out of the picture. I can only guess what they have been through. After his sudden departure, I know they had to uproot themselves and create a new life. I want to tell Carmen I had a great father and reassure her that not all

88

men are bad. I want to tell her things will get better for her.

When Ashley and Craig get back, Ashley decides we should go on something we can all ride. We head over to the Wonder Wheel, an old restored Ferris wheel. Then we go on a few other rides, most of them little kid rides Carmen can ride. I even get to go on the Cyclone with Craig one time. He laughs at me for being somewhat terrified of it. I explain the Cyclone is more unnerving because it is a wooden roller coaster. He has no idea how many accidents I have witnessed throughout my long life.

We go to the food stands and buy ourselves some giant pretzels. The crystals of salt from the pretzel dissolve on my tongue as I bite into it. We are not able to find seating, so we continue walking around. The fog has lifted, and the sun is warming my skin. We go on more of the rides and play a few of the games. Craig wins a stuffed animal for Carmen after about the third try. Seating is finally available by the time we are hungry for lunch. We buy hot dogs and soda and swoop in to get seats from a couple who have just finished eating. I take a bite of my hot dog. The juicy hot dog pairs well with the sour mustard. Carmen lifts the hot dog right out of the bun to eat it.

After lunch we all lounge under the sun on a large beach blanket Ashley brought. It's a large quilted blanket with cats hopping across the panels. Ashley is reapplying her sunscreen while chatting with Craig. I can't hear what they are saying, but they are laughing a lot. She constantly looks over to Carmen who is playing in the sand with her sand bucket and shovel. I put my head on my bag and stretch out on the blanket, eager to soak in more sun.

I try to grasp how grateful I feel. It was only a few months ago we all started hanging out together. Before, I would only share minimal small talk with my coworkers during our shifts. It seems amazing how we've gone from being acquaintances to being friends in such a short time. I'm glad the messenger's tasks ended up including Ashley and Craig instead of having to do everything alone, like I used to.

I sit up and hug my legs. I look out, through the many beach umbrellas, to where the sky and ocean meet. The weather couldn't be better, and I am more content than I have been in a while. Away from the uncertainties in life, it is nice to pause and listen to the waves crash over each other on the shore. Nearly everyone looks at ease, except for the occasional parent scolding a child for kicking up sand or barking at seagulls for stealing food. I lie back down with my bag behind my head and drift off to the sound of the waves in the distance.

17

I let out a yawn and can feel my cheeks are sunburned, which is okay since it will be gone in a few hours anyway. We are following Craig to the subway station, trying not to get separated in the crowd. We decided we wanted to get back to Manhattan so we wouldn't have to take the subway back in the dark. It's better not to take that risk. I rub my eyes as I try to keep up; the nap made me groggier than before.

We follow Craig up the stairs to the elevated subway and wait with a crowd of people. Usually there would not be so many people around on a weekend day, but everyone had the same idea to come to Coney Island for the start of their vacation. They all seem to be leaving at once, after a long day of rides, junk food, and time on the beach. There are a group of college students in their NYU apparel, a couple families with young children, and a few older couples as well. There are also a few homeless men and a handful of street performers with their acts packed up at their sides. The sunlight is peeking through the overhanging structure arching over the series of tracks, and there is a cool breeze coming through. Nothing seems out of the ordinary.

Craig looks around and wears an expression of concern. "I think this is it."

"What?" I look into his eyes.

"The one in my dreams," he says before turning to Ashley. "You have to leave now, Ashley. Get Carmen out of here."

Ashley appears confused, but then her expression turns to fear. She remembers what he had said about his dream. "Yeah, okay." She takes a few steps toward the exit as a scream rings out from a distance.

A faint uproar begins at the other end of the platform. Another high-pitched scream reverberates through the station, followed by more. Little children start crying in the background, and the crowd starts to jostle us around. In a panic, people rush toward the stairs and end up knocking others over without looking back. A primal instinct for survival takes over. A man wearing black knocks me to the ground as he runs past me. I let out a moan and struggle to get to my feet. Men and women on either side of me are lumped together, stampeding toward the exit. I can't even see Ashley or Craig anymore. I call out their names, but there is no reply.

A few feet in front of me stands a lanky young man in a black hoodie that shades his eyes. He has a black bandanna covering his nose and mouth and one tied tightly around his forearm. In terror, I watch as he pulls out a machete and runs it across the abdomen of a middle-aged man. He laughs and runs off as the man grasps his bleeding stomach and collapses. My stomach lurches. I may vomit. Another man shoves past me and similarly attacks a lady ahead of me. She lets out a horrifying scream and also falls. I regain my composure and push through the crowd calling out for my friends.

The two men in black have run out of view. A train pulls in, and people scramble to push their way onto it. People continue to bump me from every direction, almost knocking me over. Ashley and Craig don't respond. My screams cannot be heard over the chaos. I continue screaming anyway.

A third man comes into view, wearing the same black clothing as the others. He runs with his machete by his side. A fountain of anger bursts through me. I use the phrase I was given by the messenger. I can barely hear myself through the

92

confusion. I am lifted into the other world of clarity. This time I can see dark and light spirits tackling each other, with many dark wisps taking over the station. This man appears to be the only hooded character left. He has a dark spirit with its tendrils tightly bound around every part of him. I shout out my second phrase. The dark tormentor lets out a shriek, and then its tendrils scatter away along with the other dark spirits near me. I experience the heaviness of my body again.

My legs are weak, and I lose my balance. My knees collide with the subway platform, and I vomit. A few minutes later I am able to get back on my feet because there is no longer a crowd, just a few lingering behind. There are a few men and women on the ground lying in their own blood. Some are unconscious, and others are in the fetal position crying out in pain. Ashley is bent over a woman with her hand on the woman's stomach. I walk over to her. We make eye contact with each other, but there are no words. I follow her around as she helps heal victims' bodies.

Craig comes over to us, very pale and out of breath. He sees what Ashley is doing and follows in silence. Ashley goes over to the last person and heals him as his family waits and watches. They are amazed and don't know what to say. Craig has a baffled look on his face. My stomach drops as it dawns on me: we are forgetting something . . . someone. Ashley's eyes widen as she turns toward Craig.

"Carmen . . . where's—"

"I . . . I don't know!"

"Where is she?!" Ashley cries, panicked.

Ashley sprints back toward the other victims. Maybe she overlooked her. She shouts out Carmen's name. I follow Ashley but move in slow motion as if my body can't keep up with my brain's request to move. Something is on the ground at the end of the platform. I move closer. The weight of dread pours over me. It's the stuffed pink bunny Craig had won for Carmen at Luna Park a few hours earlier.

I stand with Craig, numb and unable to move. We both look down at the bunny. Ashley continues to pace back and forth until she comes to where we are standing. She looks at our faces and then toward the bunny. Ashley bends over to pick it up. A flash of realization spreads across her face. She peeks over the ledge of the subway platform toward the tracks and falls onto her knees sobbing.

A few months after my accident, I was sitting with my five-year-old son Andrew on my sofa. We were in my sitting room off of my bedroom where I would get changed in the mornings but also freshen up my makeup before dinner. Andrew was the only one of my children who came to visit in the early evenings.

I pushed down some of his wild blonde locks as I read to him. My husband had brought him back a new book from town. It was a cautionary tale for children. There was a scary wolf in it that would eat children if they strayed too far from their homes or lied to their parents. The wolf had pointy teeth and sharp claws, and wore a hungry expression.

As I finished the last line of the book, Andrew's small concerned face looked up at me. His blue eyes were opened wide. "Bones isn't going to do this, is he, Mummy?"

"No, I'm sure Bones would do nothing of the sort," I said.

His eyes were almost overflowing with tears. He was very nervous and shy around our new dog, who roamed our property for our protection. One day when we were out on our daily afternoon stroll, the nervousness turned into fear when Bones playfully nipped at his fingers. At the time, I would take daily walks before our evening tea. My children had accompanied me, until they became older and less interested. Andrew still wanted time with me every day and was the last of the children still to do so.

Andrew placed his head on my lap, and I gently rubbed his back. He was still an easily frightened child, but I enjoyed our moments together. It would not last very long. He would grow older sooner than I wanted. I knew I would miss him in a few

94

years when we would have to send him away to boarding school. I tried to cherish the time I had with him while it was available. To my disbelief, it would be my daughter Scarlet with whom I would get less time.

A few months had come and gone, and I was forced to witness the tragedy of my sweet daughter Scarlet. She was only seven when she and her twin Violet came home sick. They had both visited their aunt who lived in town under quite different living conditions. If I had known that the sickness was spreading, I would have kept them home. We thought when they regained their appetite, they had overcome their sickness. But to our despair, the consumption in Scarlet's body would ravage her.

Scarlet was placed in the former nursery, away from the other children. Her governess slept in the room attached to it and would give her what she needed throughout the day. Each morning I sat in the chair beside her bed, looking down at her flushed face hot with fever and her drooping eyelids. Although a bit of a troublemaker, she once was the joy filling our home, a force of energy always running around. Her spark was being snuffed out more and more each day. Was there anything I could do to make her better? Surely the energy she had at one time could help her come back from this.

In a few days her hot face was replaced with one cold and colorless. Her body was kept in her bed until her processional was held. Violet was never the same after losing her twin sister. Most days Violet's face was solemn and downcast. It was the hardest on her. "Why did Scarlet have to go and not me?" Violet had once asked me. I did not have an answer.

18

I sink back into my chair as the sun falls behind the buildings of Manhattan. I'm sitting in one of the two outdoor patio chairs Patricia, our landlady, bought for the rooftop of our apartment building. A small table sits between them. I crinkle my nose. The upholstery has a smoky odor. Turns out, the furniture isn't here for us; it's for her smoking breaks. The chill starts to bite at my hands. I zip up my jacket and put my hands in my pockets.

I unlock my phone. There is a text from Craig. "Almost there."

I had such a hard time today at work. Mr. Hardy was there, and he wanted me to train the new hire. I tried my best to explain to the new girl our company's policies and procedures but was constantly distracted and distant. It was a constant struggle to stay on task throughout the day. I can't even recall her name. I wish Craig had been there to talk to after what happened yesterday.

I hear the door creak open. Craig is peering from around the rooftop door. I meet him where he stands. He reaches out to hug me in a tight embrace. The soft texture of his hoodie brushes against my cheek, and I smell the pleasant scent of his cologne. A warm tear falls down the side of my face, and I wipe it away with the back of my hand. He clasps my shoulders, and his eyes look into mine, his head craning down due to his tall height. His eyes fill with tears behind his thick-framed glasses.

"I just wanted to come to make sure you were doing okay."

I nod and give him a smile, wiping away another escaping tear. I texted him after my shift and explained I needed someone to talk to. It was nice even to have someone I could text, but he insisted on being with me in person. He could probably tell how lonely I was feeling. From our chairs we watch as the city lights turn on, with the last of the orange in the sky resting on the horizon. The night seems to swallow the city minute by minute.

I can't erase the images from the subway. Ashley was sobbing on the platform and yelling out in agony. She jumped down onto the tracks and raced to put her hands onto Carmen's motionless, crumpled body on top of the tracks. During the middle of the confusion, a train had come in, probably right after Carmen was thrown down onto the tracks.

Craig called the police and ran to find an employee to tell them to stop any incoming trains on the track. There was nothing I could do besides watch Ashley bent over crying, her hands on Carmen's body. She rested her hands on Carmen the way she would when healing, but nothing happened. Ashley was soon wailing, and the medics who came a while later had to tear her away. They took Carmen's body away under a white sheet. I held Ashley as she cried on my shoulder with her arms tightly wrapped around me, some of Carmen's blood still on her hands and clothes.

The cops came and asked us different details about what had happened. Ashley's and Craig's stories were similar to mine. We overheard a few people say their injuries disappeared in a miraculous way, with the residual blood serving as proof they had been injured. The police were confused by this but focused more on what had happened to Carmen. I was relieved no one, as far as I knew, outright mentioned Ashley as the one who had healed them.

None of it made much sense. It appeared as if the men who

were attacking people were doing it for sport. There wasn't something to be gained from it, like money or revenge as in some of the other cases. Especially with what they did to Carmen. What sick twisted pervert would throw a young girl onto train tracks? After all my years, after all the destruction and violence the world has witnessed, I still can't wrap my mind around it.

After we were interviewed at the subway station, we brought Ashley back to her apartment and sat with her for a few hours. None of us could eat anything even though we hadn't eaten since lunch. Ashley kept asking how it could have happened and why she wasn't there to stop it. She kept asking herself aloud, but there were no answers. I am an adult, a smaller adult, but I was still pushed to the ground on the platform. We were all separated from each other, and distracted by the uproar.

I wish I could have told her I knew what it was like to lose people you love. If I had said anything, it would have felt contrived. After all, I tell everyone I am an only child with two living parents. Would I have to make up a grandparent I lost in order to illustrate the point? Even then, not all grandchildren are close to their grandparents. It's different losing a mother, father, or sister. It was harder than ever to have to lie. If I ever gained enough courage to tell them the truth, how could I ever convince them of my real identity? They might never trust me again.

Ashley's mom came home at around nine o'clock. Craig and I were huddled around Ashley with solemn expressions on our faces. I tried to smile, but it failed to look sincere.

"Did you see any of my calls?" Ashley asked her mom.

"What's wrong, Ashley? I was so busy at work; I wasn't checking my phone. What happened? You're scaring me."

Ashley put her face in her hands and mumbled to us that she needed to be alone with her mom. Craig and I got up from the couch in a slow, awkward sort of way. We said our good-byes. I felt as if I was allowing my body to move but didn't know how I was doing it. Craig and I walked down the stairs and out to the street. He insisted on walking me to my apartment before heading home. We promised to be in touch soon and to check in on Ashley.

"I recognized those men, you know," Craig said, interrupting my thoughts.

"From where?"

"Well, not in person but on the news. Sometimes they play the local news in our study lounges in the student buildings. I thought the reports said they were more into vandalism than anything else. Like breaking into cars and stuff."

"You sure it was the local news?"

"Yeah, and they had bandannas just like that. People are calling them the Notorious Gang. It seems like they are only active in Manhattan."

Why would this gang have turned to more extreme violence, killing people in the process?

Craig curses and takes off his glasses to rub his eyes. He wipes his glasses off with the bottom of his hoodie. "I'm such an idiot."

"What do you mean?"

"What good are these dreams if they are so vague?"

"Come on, we were able to help a lot of people because of your dreams." I try to be encouraging.

"Yeah, I guess. We should have just insisted on staying away from any subway station until the dream went away, or at least with Carmen . . . I should have known."

"I didn't do so well either. I went into the spirit world only after seeing the third guy dressed in black. The other two managed to get away."

Craig lets out a sigh. "That sucks. I don't mean you . . . we both have been off these past few days."

"I hope Ashley knows we tried our best..."

"In time she will come around," Craig says, although I don't know if he truly believes it.

I give him what I hope is a reassuring smile. Craig gives a half smile back and leans back into his chair. The sun is now completely below the horizon, leaving behind darker shades of blue. A few stars shine from above, not as visible in the city sky. The buildings of different sizes and shapes tower over the streets below, more lights being turned on inside them.

I wasn't hesitant in doing what the messenger had told me to do the first day we met in the coffee shop. I understand now it was because there wasn't much risk. I kept to myself and didn't have anyone close enough to care much about. I lived like a hermit to make sure things stayed that way. The dynamics have changed. In a way I'm glad, but it's also unnerving because I now have people I care about again, people I could lose.

"I had a younger sister once," Craig says as he looks over at me.

I stay silent and wait for him to continue.

"There was an accident when I was really young . . . I loved going outside in the backyard during the summer with my sisters. Our parents bought us a lot of toys so we wouldn't get bored. We liked playing with our sidewalk chalk, bubbles, and our tree house. We even had a tree swing."

When he says this, my mind flashes back to my backyard adventures with Anne and our favorite oak tree, our swing, and our poorly constructed tree forts.

"On the really hot days, we would swim in the pool. My older sisters liked diving for pool toys. Looking back, I think my mom was really tired that day from keeping up with us. She reclined in one of the pool chairs with her floppy hat and the home magazines she always read to pass the time. My two older sisters were in the deep end trying to see how fast they could get the sinking toys from the bottom. I was in the shallow end, watching my three-year-old sister who was in her floaty wings near the steps."

I felt a heaviness inside as I could guess where the story was going.

"I wanted to go swim in the deep end but didn't. Instead, I went under the water a few times with my goggles on trying to watch my sisters from the shallow end. What I didn't know was my little sister had taken her wings off. When I understood

100

what had happened, it was too late. She was floating on her stomach, her lungs already filled with water. I called out for my mom a few times before she responded. When she looked up, she rushed to grab her from the water and tried to do CPR on her tiny chest. My mom asked one of my sisters to run into the house to call 911. I had never seen my mom so bewildered. There was nothing any of us could do. It was too late."

"I'm really sorry. That sounds really terrible," I say, wanting to give him a hug. Considering how much he jokes around at work, I never would have guessed he had experienced a tragedy like that. I want to tell him I know that awful feeling and have experienced it many times. Those who pass away are never really gone. They are tied to the memories of the living. I hope he doesn't blame himself for it.

"I can't help but think . . . would things be different if I'd watched her like I was told? Would I still have a little sister?"

I put my hand on his shoulder. "Don't be too harsh on yourself. You didn't know." Those thoughts chew away at your insides if you let them.

"Every time I have one of my dreams, I try to pay attention to the people in them. Who are they? Are they not only a pedestrian, businessperson, or homeless person but also a sister, a father, or an aunt? What are their hopes and dreams for the future? Will they no longer have a future? I think about my little sister, Laura, and what school she would have gone to and what career she would have chosen if she hadn't died."

I nod, offering a comforting expression. It's clear he's been dealing with this for a while. He now has a purpose in doing something with his gift rather than just watching events from his dreams come to pass. But Craig will probably continue to question himself for a while, wondering if he could have saved Carmen like he wishes he could have saved Laura.

We sit in almost complete silence, with the cold air breezing past us. I study the lights from the buildings and the stars. I tuck my legs in a crossed position. The cushy chair supports my back. My nose is becoming used to the smoky smell of the chairs. There is something reassuring about sitting next to someone you know and trust even if words are not exchanged. A sort of comfort rests between us, even in our thoughts about yesterday. I soak in everything I see and hear around me. I am glad Craig trusts me enough to tell me stories of his life, and I hope someday I can do the same.

19

It is a sunny Tuesday with a few clouds in the sky, but there is no time to enjoy the weather. The day before, I had another training session with the new girl and had to lock up the store at the end of our shift. I must have seemed distracted still; hopefully I wasn't too rude. I am glad she is not coming in today. I don't enjoy putting in effort to be polite and seem put-together when I'm not feeling it.

I watch Ashley as she organizes jewelry on the front desk and in the glass case. I put a few of the clothes away from the go-back rack. They were put aside by a lady who couldn't decide what she wanted to wear. Ashley lets out a sniffle every now and again, and her eyelids are puffy. She is wearing no makeup; her hair is dirty and pulled up in a sloppy bun. She is wearing an old pair of ripped pants and a hoodie. I'm surprised she came back to work already. Then again, it is hard to take time off work when you live in an expensive place like Manhattan. Maybe it's a good distraction for her rather than sitting at home. Craig comes out of the back holding a small box.

"I think this is the right one," he says as he sets the box down on the desk.

"Yeah, this is the one," she replies after she looks inside the box. She starts replacing some of the jewelry where the jewelry racks are bare.

"Do you need help going through it?" I ask her, peering inside the box of jewelry.

"No, it's okay."

"Are you sure? I can—"

"It's fine." Ashley gives me a serious look, and I back away toward the clothing section. Craig waits nearby, watching Ashley with concern. I hope he doesn't say anything and can just give her some space for a few minutes.

"Look, we are only here to help. We—"

"Yeah, like how you helped in the subway station." Ashley glares at him and then at me. Craig and I stand in place, not sure what to say. Craig looks down as if in remorse.

She looks up at me. "All those other times you made those criminals stop in this 'other world,' but then you suddenly couldn't do it then? How is that?" Ashley is fuming.

"I . . . I . . ." I am stunned and can't find any words to say. All explanations I could give leave my mind.

Craig comes to my defense. "Come on, Ashley. That's not fair. She didn't know when it was coming."

Ashley is still fuming, glaring at us.

Craig can't meet her gaze. "If anything, we should have convinced you not to bring her."

"No, don't you blame this on me! You are the one who should have known when and where it would happen. After all, isn't that what your dreams are? The future? You said you had a dream about it. Why didn't you tell us to get out of there sooner?

"I . . . I didn't know," Craig says, looking defeated.

Ashley moves away from him, and her anger turns into tears, her arms propping up her body hunched over on the counter. Her sobs make her shoulders shake. Craig reaches over to try to comfort her.

"Don't touch me!" Ashley lashes out and knocks his hand back, sending a pile of jewelry to the floor. She pushes the front door so hard the bell rings violently, and in the next moment she is gone.

I remember the year 1924 when I was living in Brooklyn. I lived in an apartment with a woman named Helen. Every week we would visit an underground club run by a friend of hers. We dressed up in our beaded dresses, pearls, and low-heeled shoes. Before each event we would stand in front of her full-length mirror and help each other pick out the perfect accessories to attract as much attention as we could.

Helen and I had met a few years prior at our previous factory job where we sewed American flags. As much as I enjoyed working with her, I was so glad when I was able to find something else. She had helped me find another job by introducing me to the agent her father worked for. I auditioned for a small film, and even though I had no experience, the agent said there was something alluring about me he could not pass up.

After my first film, I acted in a second film even more popular than the first one. I was still waiting to hear about the release of my third film. I changed my image so even my previous coworkers would not recognize me. My hair was in a bob ending right below my ears, which at first made my neck feel bare. Helen had also found a better job as a receptionist. Even though I was gaining more prestige, I would forever be grateful to Helen and would continue to cherish her friendship.

On this night, we were let into the speakeasy by one of Helen's male friends. I could smell the heavy clouds of smoke and hear the light tunes of jazz music as he opened the door for us. There was something contagious about the laughter, the shoes shuffling on the dance floor, and the clinking of glasses. The middle of the wooden floor was full of couples dancing with beads and feathers bobbing up and down. The edge of the dance floor was skirted by small round tables were men and women would take a break from dancing to chat and drink. The jazz band was made of three men playing the saxophone, trumpet, and bass. They took turns with improvised solos. The trumpet player leaned back to push out the last note of his solo, followed by an applause from those seated. On the other side of the room, there was a long table where a man was serving drinks to the guests. Everyone seemed to be having a great time. With each dance, they watched their troubles melt away, if only for one night.

I sat down at one of the small tables, and Helen ran off to the corner where she recognized a group of men, whom we saw there almost every time we came. There were always several familiar faces as well as a few new ones. There was one handsome man named Frank who had greased-back jet-black hair, kind eyes, and an adorable smirk. His eyes held a memorable twinkle in them. I had told him to look for me this evening. After a minute of scanning the crowd, I spotted him across the room talking to a small group of people. I sat down and could not bring myself to make my way to him. Frank was compassionate and gentle but also spontaneous and carefree. He wanted to hear my opinions and wanted to be around me for who I was, unlike other men who only saw me as an upcoming star, someone they should associate with.

An aching guilt in me continued to bubble up, even though I had worked so hard to push it back. It was an unrelenting wave in a storm. My husband's face and the feeling of his arm linked in mine continually came to my mind. My children's faces glared at me. I knew there was nothing I could do. They were gone. I kept pretending I could start over if I changed my name, my clothes, or my hair, but their memories were always with me, always haunting me. If I continued to see Frank, I would only be ripped open from the inside and would take him down with me.

I sat at the same table the whole night. I decided then and there I would have to live my life as a bystander. I continued to watch people dance, most of them now in a drunken stupor. Some flailed their limbs out on the dance floor and laughed without reason, while the music they danced to became eerie and far from comforting. They tried distracting themselves from the worries they heard in silence, but they were instead killing themselves a little each day. They would continue to try and numb the pain rather than confront their issues, and act without fear of the consequences just like their grandparents and those before them.

A younger gentleman asked for my autograph, followed by several the next hour. I began to notice my popularity was becoming more than I had cared to admit. I was saddened at the thought of what I knew I had to do. Poor Helen would get over it eventually, though I knew it would take her a while.

Helen would unlock the door tonight and maybe notice something was off but not know what. She would slump over in her comfy chair for about an hour. Then she would probably be awakened by something outside and make her way to her bedroom. She would open my bedroom door to see if I had made my way back earlier, and find my clothes, blankets, and trinkets gone.

20

I sit next to Craig in the small funeral home, fifth pew back. I look down at my hands in my lap. I'm wearing a dark purple dress I have not had the excuse to wear in a while, a black cardigan, pantyhose I bought a few days ago, and short-heeled black shoes. Craig is wearing a black blazer with slacks and a buttoned-up dress shirt. Given any other occasion, I would have noticed how stunning he looks dressed up. We are both watching groups of people come in and sit down. An easel at the front displays Carmen's picture, and next to it sits a small table with a bronze urn on top. I still can't believe she is gone. I can imagine her giggling and bouncing around, with Ashley trying to calm her down. There are also different collections of bouquets on the slightly raised stage. Somehow they managed to put together a ceremony in only two weeks after the accident. How hard it must have been for the family to make arrangements on top of dealing with their grief as well as the unresolved police investigation.

Craig and I have both tried texting Ashley, but she hasn't responded to any of our messages. I've also noticed there haven't been many shifts Ashley has worked with us. I can imagine she requested to be scheduled for days and times neither Craig nor I would be working. Over the last few days,

I have given up on texting her and wasn't sure if there was anything I could say to make her answer. Craig told me about the memorial a few days ago.

"Did she answer your texts yet?" I ask Craig.

"No . . . none of them," he said, looking glum.

"How did you know about the service then?"

"Her mom sent me and my family an email about it. My family couldn't come."

"How long have your families known each other?" I ask, trying not to sound too nosy.

"It's been a few years now. I carpooled with Ashley when we went to school together. Our families became friends."

"Oh, okay. Cool." Maybe this is why they've always seemed so comfortable with each other. I try to push away these distractions and turn my attention to the printed program I was handed at the door.

"Thanks for coming to get me," I tell Craig, who is also looking at his program. He met me outside my apartment this morning. I am thankful he'd hopped off his bus so we could get on one together. I might not have had the courage to take one here alone.

"No problem." He looks into my eyes searching for something else to say.

Almost all the guests are seated, with a new person coming in here and there. Ashley and her mom come in from the side, stopping the conversation they were having with a couple. A few other close family members sit with them in the front row. I wonder how they are related. Maybe uncles, aunts, and cousins?

The slideshow on the screen begins to play, showing different moments from Carmen's life. It starts out with a young Ashley sitting on a couch holding baby Carmen in her arms with a wide smile. Another picture shows Carmen in a diaper and Ashley lying on the ground, both of them coloring together in coloring books. Then they are both standing on a porch wearing matching outfits and backpacks in what looks like a first-day-of-school picture. In the next one, they are with their mom at a pumpkin patch holding pumpkins. Almost every photo has either Ashley or her mother in them. There are other memories of Easter, Christmas, and Thanksgiving through the years.

A lump catches in my throat as I see Ashley and Carmen on the screen holding out their wrists decorated with the friendship bracelets they made. I remember holding Carmen's little hand and seeing how her face lit up when she told me about making those bracelets with her sister. I had no idea at the time it would be my last conversation with her. It brings me back to when my oldest daughter Bethany was so excited to have a little sister. Lily was more timid as a little girl, so Bethany would hold her hand and lead her. They held hands wherever they went. In the same way, Ashley had been a constant support for Carmen, always there for her when she needed her. For Ashley, there will be a hole left in Carmen's place, impossible to fill.

It was 1837 and I was sitting next to Edmund with my hands in my lap. We had only been married a few months, and I was still getting adjusted to my new living arrangements. I felt the hardwood seat underneath me and the stiffness of my dress keeping me up straight. My sisters and their husbands sat beside us in the front row, with my mother sitting at the end. A few rows of family and friends all sat behind us in the guest parlor of my childhood home. I looked at the coffin in front of us. It had been shut after our viewing and would remain closed forever. This was the last I would ever see of my father.

It seemed as though he was right after all. I had thought it was ridiculous I was encouraged to marry someone I barely knew. I never told my father I was resistant to the idea, but he could somehow see it in my eyes. He would reassure me again and again it would work out, especially during my first introductions to Edmund. My father always asked if Edmund was treating me with respect. I assured him he was. All those nights of wasted tears. I was crying over something I thought might or might not happen. My father was able to come to my wedding, although I was never able to tell him how much I was glad they picked Edmund as their choice, despite my hesitation in the beginning.

I glanced down at my black dress, trying to hold in my tears as I listened to the sound of the violin being played near the front. I placed my hand on my stomach. My hand rested on the slight bump barely visible under my dress. I was not very far along then, and not too many people knew. The thought kept playing over and over in my head: my children would never get to meet my father. He would have been a terrific grandfather.

I smelled a horrible odor and tried not to vomit, like I did most mornings then. I tried to focus on the glow of the candles set on a few small tabletops and the massive flower arrangements of lilies surrounding the casket. Edmund gave my hand a squeeze and gave me a half smile. I was grateful that I had his support. It made everything easier to deal with. We had come such a long way in a few months.

21

The slideshow fades to black on the screen, and the houselights come back on. The presenter introduces each family member before they come up to the stage. Ashley and Carmen's mom is the first one to speak. She pulls out a piece of paper, and her hand trembles. A lump forms in my throat as she stops midsentence, trying to compose herself. Her mom manages to say the last of her written words but not without tears. A man sitting in the front row helps her down from the stage.

Ashley begins her speech after she is introduced. She manages to keep a level voice, sounding rehearsed, but I can see her hands shaking.

"When Carmen was born, I was so excited to be a big sister. No matter how many times she pulled my hair or puked on me, she would always make me smile. I taught her how to tie her shoes, even though she preferred her laceless shoes, and how to jump rope. We even threw costume parties with our dresses, plastic beads, and blue eye shadow, and stayed up late with her listening to the scary stories I would read to her." Ashley goes on to tell a few more stories about Carmen.

Ashley seems to look in my direction but then snaps her focus to the back of the room. "Thank you, Carmen, for all you were to me in our short time together. I will hold on to these moments for the rest of my life."

A couple family members follow her with their own memories of Carmen before we are released. During the closing statements, we are all invited to go to a nearby restaurant after passing our condolences to the family.

A few older couples line up near the front where Ashley and her mom are standing. We stand in the line behind them, hoping our presence will be comforting. Craig looks through his program, and I wrap a strand of hair around my finger, fidgeting. After a few minutes, we are almost to the front of the line. When Ashley sees us, her face drops into a glare. She whispers something to her mom before storming off. I want to follow her, but I'm afraid it won't do any good, especially here. I don't want to make a scene. Craig sees and gives me a look of disappointment.

Despite Ashley leaving, Craig still wants to talk to her mom. We get to the front of the line, and Craig asks if there is any way we can help out and how sorry he is about what happened. Her mom says that they are doing okay, or as well as they can be given the circumstances. We each give her a hug, then walk toward the front door to exit. Craig suggests the two of us go to a different lunch place than everyone else, and I agree.

As we walk out, I notice the men and women in small clusters talking to each other. Most are wearing spring outfits, with the women in floral tops or dresses and the men in short-sleeved button-downs. I notice an older man wearing a peacoat and hat. I have never seen him before, but the style of coat he is wearing is familiar. The subway incident comes to my mind. I remember a black peacoat, in the chaos, flashing by as the three men in black came through. I pause after we exit the double doors; my feet are frozen.

"What? What is it?" Craig notices I have fallen behind.

"We were being followed."

"Huh? When?"

"That day at Coney Island . . . the jazz man and his men were following us from the time we left Manhattan that morning." I know the police are looking for Carmen's killers, but who are they compared to the dark creatures in the spirit world? They would never stand a chance.

22

My burger and fries are placed in front of me. The waitress smiles and says, "Enjoy," before taking off to her next table. They smell delicious, and my mouth starts watering. I have always been accustomed to eating every meal, despite my body not really needing it. I wouldn't die if I didn't get food; it would just leave me feeling uncomfortable. My body still gives me some signals of hunger pains and drowsiness, as if it doesn't understand I can outlive such things which used to be necessities. Either way, I am glad I can still enjoy the flavors of food.

Both Craig and I take big bites of our burgers. It tastes less fulfilling than it would under other circumstances. The image of Carmen and Ashley wearing their friendship bracelets and the way Ashley glared at us and walked away won't leave my mind. Where will we go from here? How can the three of us make amends? I don't know how Craig and I can chase the evil in his dreams if Ashley is not with us, or if I even want to. These altercations we have been up against have put all of us in potential danger. There is nothing we can do for Carmen now, but maybe I can still save them.

I scan the restaurant as I take more bites. The booth seats are a bright red, and the flooring is a black-and-white tile, with the windows almost reaching the height of the ceiling. On each table bottles of ketchup and mustard sit next to the napkin holders. There are a few couples sitting on bar stools, and the waitresses rush around in their knee-length white dresses, plastering their faces with smiles that plead for tips. I half expect them to be wearing roller skates as I would have seen in the sixties, but I'm reminded that was more than a few years ago. I tend to like places like these. They bring me back to another time in my life. I continue to eat very slowly as Craig talks in between bites.

Craig and I discuss how we might be able to help out Ashley and her mom in their time of grief. We consider bringing them a few meals so they don't have to cook or get food for themselves.

"I remember Carmen showing me her bracelet . . . the one they showed in one of the pictures. It was only a few hours before she . . . I just keep asking myself, did we do all we could do?" I wait for an answer.

"I know. I feel it too." Craig shakes his head. "One day, even if not right away, Ashley will see we really did all we could."

"After all that we've seen in Manhattan, I didn't want to believe the jazz man would seek me out again. I know he was there in the past, but now it seems like he can have anyone he wants come after us. I had thought Carmen was accidentally bumped onto the tracks, but now I'm thinking the jazz man threw her."

"Maybe we should double our efforts, causing him to become too weak to do anything to anyone," Craig suggests.

"No, I don't think aggravating him more will help. If we leave him and his followers alone, he won't have a reason to attack us again." I'm reminded that every cursed spirit in Levizar's region is under his command.

"But that is what they want. They want us to be afraid. What about those people you said we need to help?"

"I just . . . I can't," I say with more force than I intend. I swallow hard, trying to keep my tears from falling. I can't

116

manage to tell him I would hold myself responsible if he or Ashley got hurt. Where were these guardians the messenger had spoken of? Did they watch Carmen while she died? I should have never trusted the messenger.

Craig opens his mouth as if to say something but remains silent. We continue eating the last of our meals without saying much. Each comment is made like small talk between strangers. The summer plans we thought so highly of only a few weeks ago are now gone from our minds. Each response is left with a long, awkward silence between us. I hope he is not ashamed of me. I want him to see things the way I do. It's better if we don't involve ourselves. There have always been events around us we will never be able to change.

We pay for our meals and walk out of the diner. "Are you okay taking the bus back by yourself?" Craig asks me.

"Yeah, thanks." I give him a forced smile. I watch him walk off in the direction of his subway station until I can no longer see him in the distant crowds of people.

Across the street, a man is grabbing a woman's purse. She screams at him while fighting to hold onto it. She yells for someone to stop him when she is no longer able to hold on, and he runs down the street with it. The woman runs about half a block before she bends over, heaving and unable to continue the chase any longer. I remind myself these things happen all the time. These reassurances don't stop the sense of guilt creeping up in me as I sit on the bus stop bench, doing nothing.

I pretended to read a newspaper I was holding while playing with my string of pearls. It was 1921 and I was on the very first film set of my acting career. I tried to ignore the goose bumps running up my neck. I still was not used to the bob haircut my agent insisted I wear.

I sat on a sofa next to a small end table with a patterned rug underneath my feet. This side of the room was staged to look like a living room, with two false walls for the entrance and exit. The small crew stood behind the camera, waiting to film my performance. From where they stood you could see the cozy living room was really just a few feet of furniture and decor placed in a room with a high industrial ceiling and many windows to the outside.

"Action!" yelled the director.

Even though I did not look up, I could hear Bill entering through the false wall. Bill was a middle-aged man who looked several years younger than he was, having lost none of his charm in aging. He wore his dark brown hair greased back and had a thin mustache. He played my husband on set. Bill lit up his cigarette when he got to his mark in between me and the false wall. I stood up and gave an exaggerated stomp with my heel as his character ignored my presence. He took drags from his cigarette and let out plumes of smoke. I waved a scarf in his face and could image the title card would fill in my silent dialogue with "Who does this scarf belong to?"

"Cut!" yelled the director. "Now, ya really gotta look angry. Your husband is no good. He's cheating. Get angry! Let's start again from the top." I nodded and sat back down.

We started the scene again, and I tried my best to exaggerate the waving of the scarf in Bill's face.

"No, get angry," the director interrupts. "It looks like you're trying to dance with it. Do it again!"

I tried not to sag my shoulders, feeling defeated on the inside. Instead of going back behind the false wall, Bill grabbed me and pulled me close. He let one hand travel down further and gave me a squeeze from behind. I rolled up my newspaper and hit him in the face with it, hard, and then a few more times for good measure.

Bill laughed at me. "Yeah, that's what it should look like!"

My face became hot with anger, but I restrained my emotions. I wished I could have punched him in the face. If the rumors about Bill were true, I didn't think I would like working with him. He liked pushing his limits on the female actresses he worked with.

I sat on the sofa again to restart the scene, trying to ignore the feelings of dejection and rage. As much as I was embarrassed by the way Bill treated me, I was even more embarrassed knowing I wasn't giving the director the delivery he wanted. My agent told the director wonderful things about me I was not sure were entirely true. What if I couldn't be the actress he wanted me to be? I would most likely let them all down no matter how hard I tried. I had quit my other job sewing flags with Helen, so there was no going back. I had to make this work somehow.

23

It is almost the end of another week. We only have about an hour left of work. I only worked with Ashley one other time besides today since the memorial. I see the new girl, Kristen, holding a stack of hanged clothing with a look of confusion on her face. She looks up and down the wall and is pacing. I finally remembered her name after a few shifts. Kristen is a small, shy girl with a little voice and a blonde bob. She still wears skirts and fancy flats like most newcomers do the first few weeks. I gave up on looking my very best for work after my first week. I point up to one of the top racks in the middle of the wall.

"Those pink ones go here." I try my best not to sound condescending. It's only been a few days since the new summer selection went up. Most of the older clothing is now on the clearance racks toward the back.

"Thanks," Kristen says, barely audible. Kristen continues slowly putting the rest of her stack back. Ashley is arranging a few new pieces of jewelry in the case. Besides her greeting at the beginning of our shift, she hasn't talked to us. Talking isn't necessary, as I know the routine for our shifts down to the last detail. We were sorting through the jewelry inventory the last time Carmen was in the store. Is Ashley thinking the same thing?

Walking to one of the round racks in the center of the store, I place my last stack of purple suit coats in their place. I see something small near the back corner of the store resting on the floor. I walk closer to make out what it is. We sometimes neglect the corners of the floors when we clean. I pick up the small plastic doll, about the size of my hand, wearing a crop top and skirt. Its hair is tangled. My heart drops as I remember Carmen holding this doll when she was playing in the store. Ashley had scolded her for snagging a piece of jewelry for her doll to wear. Should I give the doll to Ashley? It might upset her more. I put it in my pocket, for now anyway, and continue working.

A few minutes pass, and Kristen and I have put away all the clothes. Ashley is sitting on a stool at the counter flipping through one of her magazines. I use the opportunity to ask Kristen more about herself. I ask her the usual questions you ask someone you don't know. The small talk I usually dread I now welcome as a distraction. I was too distant on our first few shifts together to even bother, but now we have less than an hour from our shift ending. Kristen tells me she lives in an apartment with her family in the area. She plans on going on a few local trips over the summer. I'm glad she seems more comfortable talking to me and uses a more moderate volume in her voice.

Ashley shuts her magazine and lets out a big yawn. After a while she looks up and tells us it is time to lock up and go home. I walk over behind the counter where she is standing. With each step, the doll presses up against me from my pocket. I stand near Ashley in silence.

"What is it?" Ashley looks at me, this time not in disgust like at the memorial.

I lift the doll out of my pocket and outstretch my hand. "Here."

Ashley sets her magazine and store keys on the counter. She takes the doll and studies it. A recognition comes over her face. Her face crinkles up. I jolt a little as she throws her arms around me and starts crying on my shoulder in loud sobs. I rest

121

my hands on her back. She remains in my arms for a few minutes before pulling back.

"I'm sorry." Her words carry more than she can say.

"I'm sorry too." I hold her close again, unable to find any other words of comfort.

24

Ashley and I walk next to each other down the street. The sky is blue with a few white clouds and a slight breeze. The windows on the buildings shimmer in the sun. We had said our good-byes to Kristen and locked up the store when Ashley offered to have me over for some leftover pasta. I trace the area on my neck where the jazz man held me in his constricting grasp. Ashley was willing to risk her reputation in healing me when I came over that day. She tends to talk more than I care to hear, but we now walk in silence.

Taking out her keys from her purse, Ashley unlocks her front door, and I find a place to sit on the couch. She sets down her purse and excuses herself to start heating up the pasta. There are a few dirty plates stacked on the table and a few piles of junk mail, but the apartment is surprisingly more cleaned up than the last time I came. There are no longer toys or coloring books spread out on the floor. I notice a few labeled boxes piled up in the corner of the living room. There is one labeled "Dollhouse" and another that reads "Tea Set." Maybe it's easier for them to cope if they have some of Carmen's things put away.

"Here you go," Ashley says as she hands me a glass of ice water.

"Thanks."

Ashley comes back a few minutes later with two plates of heated spaghetti with sauce and small pieces of garlic bread. She sets our plates down on the coffee table in front of us and sits next to me. As we eat, I tell her about a show I've found to watch.

"I was watching this reality show about this woman who helps people figure out what they should wear. She goes through their closet and takes out all the hideous outfits."

"Yeah, I know about that one."

"They go shopping for new outfits, but the people being made over still put up a fight. Somehow, the hostess always seems to make them look and feel better by the end of the show. You remind me of her. You could totally do her job, helping out the city one confused person at a time."

Ashley lets out a laugh. "It sounds like a frustrating job, but I'd be up for it! I want to show you some of the outfits I made for the contest a while ago." We put down our plates and I follow her to the clothing rack.

"I didn't mean to put it on you and Craig," Ashley says as she pulls a blouse off the rack.

"I understand. I wish I had seen it coming, and then maybe I would have acted faster. Craig feels terrible too that he didn't have you take Carmen away first. I know he was worried about not knowing exactly where it would happen."

Ashley nods and turns her gaze to the floor. "And I should have listened. It wasn't fair to Carmen. I just . . . I keep thinking that . . ."

"I know. Something could have been done differently."

"The crowd came around us so fast . . . I should have held on tighter to her hand."

"We were all feeling lost." The panic of the crowd around me still echoes in my memory.

"I still can't believe it . . . I always told myself, when we were older, I could be more like a sister again . . . less like a parent."

I wait for her to talk, careful not to give her any advice but instead to look into her eyes as she speaks. I witnessed how much of a mother figure Ashley was for Carmen. Any word of comfort from me now may feel like I am brushing off her concerns.

"I think I hear her in the other room sometimes . . . but then I remember. I wish we had never gone to Coney Island. It's just . . . I don't know." Ashley's eyes look heavy.

"I remembered the other day he was there . . . the jazz man. He followed us from Manhattan to Coney Island with his men."

Ashley's eyes widen.

"Those men were the Notorious gang members the jazz man and other spirits are in control of . . . and they cut through people like it was nothing." I recall the noises the men and women made as they fell.

"That's really scary."

"I knew the jazz man, or Levizar, was over the cursed spirits in this region, but I had no idea he had such a direct control over them. Somehow they were able to move outside their region to follow us."

Ashley stares at the ground with her eyes still wide.

"I don't want to get involved anymore if I can help it, though," I continue. "It doesn't seem worth it. I want them to leave us alone. When will they ever stop? I was only able to get one of the curse spirits from their group. The others are still out there."

Ashley nods and takes a sip of her water.

"Don't worry, Craig and I will be here for you whenever you need us to be."

"Thanks. That's means a lot, it really does."

25

I see myself sitting in the dark. I sit on my couch under my loft bed. My face glows with the light from the blaring television. My expression is blank as I munch on popcorn from a bowl. My cat, Cosmo, sits next to me also watching. I turn to Cosmo who is making deep growling noises. His pupils enlarge, and he pricks his ears. In my peripheral vision I see a shadow next to me on the couch. I turn my head toward it. It is holding a small stuffed bunny. "Do you want to play with me?" the shadow says. Its small frame is bent over in a twisted way with contorted limbs. Its small legs kick up and down at the edge of the couch. Its body mimics a disfigured version of Carmen's. Its face turns toward mine wearing Carmen's smile but with totally black eyes.

I want to move but am frozen. The shadow laughs at me with a girl's laugh that turns into a deep cackle. It grabs my shoulders with its talon fingers, and its black eyes come closer to mine. Its hands inch toward my throat and then start to tighten around my skin. Suddenly the shadow is wearing a nightgown. The face turns into Scarlet's, my sick daughter I couldn't make well. It coughs, spewing blood in my face and down its chin. "Why didn't you save me?" she says, with both the voices of Carmen and Scarlet in unison. I dart up and run as fast as I can toward the bathroom. But it's as if I am running in slow motion. I get to the bathroom before the shadow and slam the door behind me. I lean against the inside of the door in relief. I glance up at the mirror and can faintly see myself in the moonlight from outside. I push my hair back to find my face missing.

Lurching upright in my bed, I breathe heavily and notice my pajamas are sticking to my skin with sweat. I look at the clock—I've overslept—and quickly climb down from my bed. I pick up Cosmo and give him a hug. I'm glad he looks cuter in real life. My head starts hurting, which I find odd. Normal people tend to have pills nearby to take anytime they need them, but I never need them. I find an outfit to put on and try to gather myself so I don't look like a mess.

Yesterday Ashley texted Craig and me, asking if we wanted to hang out. She was nervous, half expecting him to say no. I encouraged her to send the text anyway. After all, I was the one who was nervous after my talk with Craig at the diner. Would he ridicule me for not wanting to confront the darks forces in the spirit world? Especially after all his years of wanting to use his dreams? Would he try to convince me to do something if we came across another horrible event? How long could I continue to ignore them?

It is a busy Saturday morning, but the three of us all have the day off. I walk through the crowds of people and street performers. I study their faces as I walk past them, kicking myself for not being more aware of my surroundings in the past. My eyes are heavy, and I feel a bit disoriented from the lack of sleep. The sun is becoming hotter as it inches up the blue June sky. I scan the crowd and see a hand waving. Ashley is on her toes with her arm outstretched above her. Craig is standing next to her. I walk over and apologize for being late.

Both Craig and Ashley are holding cardboard coffee cups, and Craig is taking the last bites of his croissant. I ask them where they got their coffee. They point to a coffee and pastry stand set up in the park, and we walk over together. It dawns on me that people drink coffee to get rid of their headaches. Using one hand, I massage my two temples. I give the woman my order and hand her some cash.

"Are you feeling okay?" Craig looks at me with concern.

"Yeah, I just didn't sleep well," I reply.

127

His expression implies he's trying to determine if I'm telling the truth. I grab my mocha and bagel with cream cheese. Craig suggests we find a place to sit, noticing me trying to juggle eating while holding my coffee. Ashley points to a bench where a mother and her children look like they are about to leave. She swoops onto the bench seconds after the mother's departure and motions us over. All three of us fit snugly on the bench. I balance my coffee in between my legs while I bite into my bagel. I smell a little bit of Craig's cologne and blush.

"Is something wrong?" Craig asks me.

Unable to answer because my mouth is stuffed so full, I shake my head in response.

Craig brings up some new shows he has been watching on Chillflix and a recommended one he has yet to watch. I tell him which characters I like the best out of the ones I have seen so far. I have not heard of the new one his roommate was talking about. Ashley has seen all the shows we mention, no surprise there, and continues to bring up different theories of how they will end in the upcoming season.

I zone out as I observe a pair of young parents passing by with their toddler and newborn. A group of college students in my peripheral vision is about to walk past us. I can swear one is staring at me. My head jerks in their direction, but they are all busy in conversation, not looking at me. Then I notice an older man and his wife coming from the other direction. I'm certain she is looking at me. I turn, but she is busy talking to her husband. These situations start and stop in the same way over and over for several minutes. My headache, which had subsided with the coffee, now returns with a strong force, and then a ringing starts in my ears. I bend over and grab my head.

"What's wrong?" Craig asks.

"Here, I have some ibuprofen if you want." Ashley hands me two from her purse.

"Thanks." I take the pills and swallow them with my little remaining lukewarm coffee.

"No prob. A girl always has to keep them on her." She zips up her purse and sets it on her lap.

We sit in silence as I do my best to relax my eyes. Near my feet is a piece of gum someone left on the concrete. My boots have more scratches on them than they did a few weeks ago. A tingling creeps up the back of my neck. Someone must be standing behind me. I try to dismiss it, but the feeling lingers. I snap my head back, but no one is there. Craig gives me another look of concern but doesn't say anything. Ashley takes out her phone now buzzing. Her thumbs move rapidly, and I assume she is answering a text. She places her phone back into her pocket and explains her mom needs help running some errands this morning. Ashley apologizes for having to leave early, but we tell her we understand.

Craig and I are left alone on the bench. After a minute I ask him if he still plans to go to any of the parks or museums he had wanted to visit this summer. He says yes, and also some other restaurants he has not been to yet. We listen to the street performers for a moment. Craig takes out a flyer from his pocket and unfolds it. He hands it to me. It has a goofy cartoon sun playing a saxophone and wearing sunglasses.

"There is a music festival happening in a few weeks. I'm sure you've heard of it."

"Yeah, a street in Greenwich Village is being blocked off." I nod.

"Uh huh. Different booths and stages and stuff. Lots of people visit each summer."

"You want . . . to go?"

"Yes, but for different reasons than you think."

I wait for him to continue as my stomach becomes heavy with anxiety.

"I want to be honest this time. And if you don't want to go, it is up to you."

"What do you mean?"

He smooths the paper in his hands, as if contemplating whether he should tell me.

"You had another dream, didn't you?"

"It was awful. It was another hazy dream . . . there were stages and booths set up all along a street. It reminded me of

129

this festival. I couldn't see what was happening exactly, but people were running and screaming, terrified."

"I—"

"You don't have to answer right away. I know you said you don't want to get involved, but I don't think you really meant it. Look, I know it's hard, but sometimes you have to take a risk. Give it some thought." Craig gives my shoulder a squeeze.

I look down at my shoes. I am filled with dread knowing he will probably expect an answer soon. I can't find the words to tell him I don't ever want to return to the spirit world. It will be better for everyone if I don't get involved. Craig and Ashley are better people than I have met in decades. If I continue to fight the cursed spirits, the jazz man will find us again and try to pick them off one by one. A flash of Carmen's bunny on the platform crosses my mind. When the messenger spoke of sacrifice, was this what he meant? Would I have ever followed his instructions if I truly knew?

In front of us, two college-aged women begin shouting at each other, calling each other various four-letter words. One of the women slept with the other one's boyfriend. The blonde, who is smaller, grabs the ponytail of the brunette and yanks her down. The brunette lets out a scream.

I continue to watch them as they brawl, not making any motions to intervene. If I enter the spirit world, the cursed spirits will be clinging to them. The blonde climbs on top of the other woman and starts punching her in the face until she starts bleeding. The blonde looks around, realizing people are watching, then sprints away. The brunette lies in a fetal position on the ground, crying and holding her face.

I want to help her up and give her some comforting words. How can I comfort her, though, when I know I could have prevented her from being beaten up? I could have called off the darkness before she was hit, but I chose not to. Instead of saying anything, or even acknowledging what happened, I ignore her. It is what I must do in order not to draw attention to myself in the spirit world. The safety of my friends must come first.

Craig reaches out to the woman on the ground and helps her to her feet. She lets out a sniffle.

"Are you going to be okay?" Craig asks her.

The girl nods and hobbles away out of view.

Craig sits next to me on the bench. He turns to me as I look down at the flyer. "Let me know what you decide."

As I continue looking down, he gets up and walks away. I look up and watch Craig until he is lost in the crowd of people. How can I make him understand? I am not trying to be stubborn or unhelpful. I am doing this for them. No matter what I continue to tell myself, I cannot let go of my despair. I am only disappointing him.

I looked up at the grand building as our carriage rolled to a stop. The house sat on a vast plot of land with fields recently dusted with new snow. Edmund and I had returned from our weeks-long honeymoon after visiting several cities across Europe. I was still only eighteen and would be able to say I had a home of my own that I shared with my husband.

My mouth opened at the size and beauty of my new home. It was made of bricks with sash windows. The center of the house near the entrance was the most prominent in size with its two stories and an additional attic level flanked by chimneys on either side. Extending from the center of the home were two wings set back, each with two stories and also a basement level. Each wing had a small chimney at both ends. The front door, made of dark cherrywood, stood above a few steps and underneath an overhang supported by two white columns.

Edmund helped me out of the carriage, and I forced myself to look down, away from the view of the house, so I wouldn't trip. I laughed as he lifted me up, with great effort, and carried me across the threshold of our new home. On either side of the entryway were two rooms. Past the doorways was a staircase going up one side of the wall before it turned at the landing and headed up the opposite side. The railing was a dark wood, matching the floors. The walls were adorned in wallpaper of luscious colors of dark green and red, patterned with flowers and birds.

He introduced me to the butler and my personal maid, Louise, who would help me dress in the mornings. The other maids and members of our staff were gathered in the entrance hall to introduce themselves. I was a little overwhelmed at the amount of people I would oversee, a lot more than my parents had. I counted myself fortunate even to step into such a luxurious home.

A few days went by before my wonder at my new life turned into frustration and embarrassment. I had a good impression of Louise when I first met her. She looked to be around the same age as my mother. It sounded like she would help me figure out my new role. She did this job a little too well. I made the mistake of addressing the lower-ranking maids in person. The lady of the house typically only spoke to the staff together in the mornings. Any other time, the maids would pretend they were invisible until she left the room or unless they were summoned with a bell. Louise scolded me one morning when she found out that I had broken this custom. I had a hard time remembering when our guests would be coming, and failed to plan ahead. I also had trouble with the etiquette of how to address my guests, what to serve them, or where to place them at the table.

Some days I would keep myself in my room for hours, not wanting to address any details related to managing the household. I told the staff to leave me by myself for a certain length of time. I tried to distract myself with writing poems or sewing, but other times I just looked out the window and thought about what I would be doing if I was still in my parents' house. I pretended for a few moments I was with Anne tying together flower necklaces under our favorite oak tree. Other days I would refuse to get out of bed until the afternoon.

Those who worked for us did not know how to handle me.

I would hear them whisper, some with snide remarks and others with pity. I was letting them down. Whatever the expectation was, I fell far beneath it.

26

Again I see myself from a distance. I put another handful of popcorn in my mouth and hear it crunch in between my teeth. On the television an episode of Befriended *is playing, except it is Ashley, Craig, and me on screen, having a conversation. Ashley tells Craig I have a big crush on him. My character denies it, and a laugh track plays in the background. Several old grannies rush through the door asking a billion questions about pieces of clothing hanging on a rack in the room, which are in fact colorful pieces of trash sewn together.*

I grab another scoop of popcorn. It feels weird watching myself on TV. I look down and hundreds of large cockroaches are crawling up my arm from where the popcorn used to be a moment earlier. I toss the bowl away from me and jump up, brushing off the cockroaches in a panic. They crawl away through the vents and out the window, but I hear a hissing noise as if they are still in the room. I turn slightly and jump. The shadow of Carmen is sitting on the couch with her legs bouncing up and down. She gets off the couch and walks toward me with outstretched hands.

My feet won't allow me to move. She is about a foot away. I creep toward the door in slow motion, my legs like gelatin. I slam the door to my apartment behind me and run down the stairs. I manage to get down to the sidewalk, then rest for a minute before the door at the top of the stoop starts to creak open. I sprint in slow motion a few blocks before finding a door to hide behind.

I look around me. I'm standing in front of a dilapidated version of Sheila's Boutique. The clothes are old and gray. The shelves are dusty and lined with spiderwebs. Only a sliver of moonlight shines through. A silhouette rises from the shadows. The jazz man is playing a dissonant tune on his saxophone, with his fedora covering his face and his peacoat hiding his form. He stops playing and looks up. His eyes glow and turn completely black. "Hello, Eliza," he hisses. I turn around and yank at the doorknob in desperation. I keep tugging at it, but nothing happens. It won't open. There are tingles down my spine as the jazz man approaches from behind. The tendrils tickle my skin before they embrace me.

I scream myself awake; my heart is pounding fast. It is dark still, around three in the morning but I can't be sure. I see a shadow and a pair of glowing eyes at the foot of my bed. I am startled, frozen, until Cosmo lets out a noise. I can almost imagine him frowning at me, his ears turned back, but it's too dark to see any details. I fan myself with the shirt I'm wearing. It's covered in sweat and sticking to my skin. I grab Cosmo and hug his big furry body. He squirms away with his fluffy tail flowing behind him. Free food and lodging and he can't even let me pet him for a few seconds. I let out a sigh as he leaps down. I follow a moment later. I must sleep but am not yet comfortable getting back into bed.

I change out of my sweaty clothes into a fresh T-shirt and flannel shorts. As I approach the bathroom, I can feel a headache coming on with every step. I scold myself for still neglecting to buy some pain reliever. I will try to remember to get some next time I'm out. I rinse off my arms with some cold water and grab the towel next to me. I dodge a glance of my reflection in the mirror. My features are shadows on my face. I blink a few times, adjusting to the dark. I begin to see my eyes in more detail. It's almost as if I expect my face to disappear like it did in my dream the other day. I try my best to push the image out of my mind as I wipe my arms dry.

After much self-talk, I slip back under my covers. This previous week was filled with other equally terrifying nightmares. They all seem to be similar. My headaches are only becoming more frequent as well, and I can't help but worry. I haven't had a single headache since I was a teenager.

A pang of guilt comes over me as I recollect the different moments of distress I have been ignoring in order to avoid going back into the spirit world. The other day I saw a boy sticking candy in his pocket and walking out of the convenient store, but I looked away. On my way to work a few days ago, two men were fighting and punching each other, but I pretended not to see them. It seems as if every other day I witness something else. What would I do if I saw something worse? Could I pretend not to notice then?

My mind keeps returning to Craig's face almost a week ago when he handed me the flyer. The last thing I want is for him to be disappointed in me. He doesn't understand how much he and Ashley mean to me. I want to keep them safe no matter what. Craig doesn't realize how hard it has been for me to make and maintain relationships. He must never know. I continue to roll over, unable to find a comfortable sleeping position. I fall in and out of sleep, unable to shake off my restlessness.

27

"Do you have this blouse in a large?"

I jerk my head up at the question asked in my direction by a lady who looks about eighty years old. She is wearing a knee-length skirt, a round hat, and bright pink lipstick, smeared on one side. She is walking toward me. My eyelids are very heavy, and I am almost falling asleep standing up. My body doesn't really need the sleep to stay alive; it's the mental exhaustion that's making me so drained. My headaches are a mystery to me as much as they are a nuisance. If only I could find some comfort.

"What was that?" I ask her, trying to focus.

"For this blouse . . . do you have a large?" She is standing closer this time, holding the gray blouse in her hand. Her hand quivers as she holds it up. The pungent smell of her perfume reaches my nostrils, and I almost gag. I tell her everything we have is out on the floor already, but I will look to see if it is on another rack. I go around the store looking for the areas with gray clothing to see if we or another customer misplaced it. When the customers aren't misplacing items, they are leaving them on the floor. I almost bump into Ashley who is talking to the daughter of the old woman I am helping. The middle-aged daughter is holding some sale items in her arms to show her mother.

I sigh in frustration. I can't seem to find it. My eyes are so tired. I look up to see the elderly woman watching me. I smile, trying to reassure her, but it likely doesn't seem genuine. I hope she is not one of those super cranky customers who throws a tantrum when you can't make the impossible happen. There are goose bumps on my neck. I shiver, remembering the tendrils creeping up and constricting me in my dream. The laugh of the jazz man is branded in my memory as is the burning around my neck from his grasp. My heart beats faster. I close my eyes and control my breathing. I reach out one hand to the round rack to steady myself.

"Do you need help?" Craig asks me, appearing next to me.

"Um . . ." I can't seem to remember what I am supposed to be doing.

"You know, I'm having trouble looking busy. I could use some work." Craig gives me a wide smile, and I return it.

"Uh . . . oh yeah…I'm trying to find another gray blouse like this . . . in a large." I hold up the top the lady gave me to show him what it looks like. "They are supposed to go here." I point to the round rack with the other gray blouses.

"Let's see . . . I think I remember seeing one like that. I'd have to see what size it was, though."

I stand there in silence as he makes his way over to the go-back rack.

"Here. I actually found it." Craig hands it to me.

"Wow, I can't believe I didn't think to look there. Thanks." I stumble over my words.

"No problem. Just let me know if you need help. Any at all." Craig has my shoulders in a light grasp for a moment and looks into my eyes as he says this. His eyes search mine. He leaves to help the two women at the register as I give the woman her blouse. I'm left in a flushed state. As much as I have hidden my life from Ashley and Craig, he still sees it. Despite my efforts, I am breaking apart.

Later in the evening we are all together, sitting in a booth at the pizza place, after a long, busy week at work. The restaurant

138

is more crowded than it was a few months ago. There are small families and college students packed into the small room, more than probably allowed by the fire safety standards. It is getting warm. I slink out of my jacket and put it on top of my purse next to me on the seat. Craig and Ashley are sitting on the same side while I am across from them.

I take small sips of my soda as I run my fingers over lettering carved into the table. Ashley talks about issues she has with her mom's new boyfriend. She can't trust anyone her mom dates, especially since she believes her mom is just trying to mask her grief. It dawns on me that Carmen was with us in this same booth, fidgeting in her seat. I can tell Ashley is hurting, although she is talking about Carmen less today than in recent days. No one forgets all their firsts with loved ones and, even more so, all the firsts they have without them.

I take a big bite of my pizza, noticing I am the last one to start eating; the pizza burns the roof of my mouth. I cringe and manage not to choke on it. Drinking my soda, I remind myself, for most people it takes days for the roof of the mouth to heal. For me it takes only a few minutes.

Ashley and Craig are talking, but I'm not paying attention. An image of Craig and me laughing at the café over a month ago pops into my mind. If we could only get back to that, I think. It's dangerous imagining a relationship with Craig. After all, I was someone's wife, so how could I avoid comparing my former marriage to a new marriage to someone else? Or how could I justify a serious relationship when he would only grow old and die long before I ever did? I shouldn't waste my time or his in order to satisfy my own curiosity and interest. It would not be realistic being with Craig; I have already disappointed him anyway.

I continue to eat my pizza as I attempt to shove my self-deprecating thoughts out of my mind. To my dismay, another headache is coming on. I focus on the grease spots on my paper plate and lick the grease from my lips. My head grows heavy. I hear whispers. I turn my head in the direction they're coming from. I only see a college-aged girl flirting with a

139

muscular-looking guy. The sound stops. I turn my eyes back toward my plate, but this only makes the whispers continue. When I force myself to look away, the whispers multiply with an underlying hiss added now. My head jolts toward the noise this time, with more force than I intend. A mother is wiping the face of her little boy. The noise stops again. I try to collect myself, letting go of the tight grip I have on the cushion of the booth.

Ashley and Craig are both staring at me, this time with their conversation at a halt. They are trying to catch my gaze. I give a poor attempt at a smile and dodge my eyes away from theirs. My head is pounding. I excuse myself to the restroom. Hopefully this will help me gain some composure. I use the facilities, then scrub my hands with soap. I stare at the bubbles. How will I be able to tell them what is going on? I don't even know what is going on. How could I even begin to explain it to them? Dread spreads through me. I can't stay in the bathroom forever. They will confront me as soon as I come out.

I have nearly scrubbed my hands raw not paying attention to how long my hands were under the water. I take in a few deep, controlled breaths while I dry my hands, and then walk out. They are muttering to each other before looking up as I come closer. I sit down on my side, and they continue to stare. I should say I'm just really tired. It's partially true. Those minutes in the bathroom did little good.

I slide into the booth as Ashley is taking something out of her purse. She places a stack of papers in front of me. "I wanted to wait until after we were finished eating," Ashley says, wearing a serious expression.

The color rises in my face as I see my name, or the name they know me by, listed many times over on the top sheet of paper. The name next to my address is circled. I flip through the next pages which list my past employers and clear criminal background. It looks like a background check issued by an employer. I don't know why she would be showing me a background check if everything listed is what she believes to be true. So far, they are correctly attributed to my current life events. My heart flutters in my chest as I look at the last page. How did I miss this?

"Mara Woods . . . that is not your real name, is it?" Ashley looks into my eyes, waiting for a reply.

It was approximately four years ago. I walked up the steps covered in old snow and grabbed the railing with my gloved hand to steady myself. I made my way past the front door and took my gloves off, placed them in my coat pockets. I started up the steps of the stairwell in front of me. My hands stung from the cold chill. I continued up until I reached the fourth floor. I knocked on a numbered door appearing no different than the other ones. There was brief silence. Maybe I had the wrong number. A pale-looking man with dark circles under his eyes poked his head through the small opening in the door with the chain still in place.

"How is the weather outside?" he asked, his stare boring into me.

"There are clouds with a small chance of rain. The humidity never lifts."

The man pauses for a moment before shutting the door to unfasten the chain, then opens the door for me. I had hoped I would remember the phrase. I would have thought my memory would improve over the years to be able to recite simple phrases. Over the years this sort transaction always unsettled my nerves. I always thought of the other people who came here besides myself, most of whom likely were not law followers or do-gooders. For me this was the only way I could remain anonymous. I could not worry myself about the crimes of the others; I simply reminded myself I needed to do this, I needed to start over, for my own protection.

I followed the man down a small hall. On our right was a small kitchen with a dining room that was really part of the kitchen. There were two women seated at a table by the window. One girl was typing away on a laptop, and the other was sorting through paperwork next to a mini printer. I stood with my arms crossed and rocked back on my heels. I listened to the man make chitchat with one of the girls about some of the difficulties she was having on her end. The other girl handed him a blue folder.

"Do you have the cash?" he asked me.

I pulled out a folded stack of cash and handed it to him. He pulled out a pen and ran it across the bills. He nodded in approval and handed me the folder. I pulled out the social security card and my ID card. I gave him a forced smile. The week before, I came in to have my picture taken and to pick out an identity from three different people who had similar birth dates with my appearance age. I had thought this one was perfect because the woman was no longer alive. I could not embrace an identity if I knew someone else was still using it. It would be more like stealing than this was. She couldn't miss her identity if she was not alive. I was told this woman did not even have any immediate family left.

I thanked the man and tucked my cards into my wallet. Several minutes later I sat at a bus stop as some new snow started to blanket the ground. After several minutes the bus came, and I was grateful to be out of the snow. I walked a few blocks to the nearest public library and logged on to one of their computers. I was careful to make sure there was no one in my aisle so I would not raise any suspicions. I combed through the different information on my new name. I looked up to see who the real Mara had been. I hoped this woman had as clean of a record as the man had told me.

I was happy to find she had a clean criminal record. She also did not have any awards or outstanding achievements that would have been hard to gloss over. I made my way through the records. Over the years, I had learned how to adjust some facts so I would not have to pretend to be that person entirely. There was no way I could pretend to be from a state I had only briefly visited or never been to at all. I was almost caught many times but knew I wanted to keep my name for at least ten years before changing it. My slight accent would threaten to give me away. Now I could alter the information to add some fake workplaces and references with numbers attached to cheap throwaway phones. I no longer had any desire to remain a dishwasher. It was mindless work. The only way I could get a new job was through a believable resume and background checks with the altered information I put into the records. I typed away until I was assured everything was covered.

I erased my history on the computer and shut it down. I slipped out of the library with little notice. I made a mental checklist of what I needed to get done before the end of the day. I would need to go over to the bank to get an account with my new ID and over the next few months transfer my earnings into my new account. I also needed to get a new cell phone and start paying the bill to improve upon my new credit.

The part I was looking forward to the least was telling the family I was living with I would soon be leaving. They were the type of people who got attached. We were almost starting to get close, and it wouldn't have been long before they started asking more questions about who I was. I wished I could leave before Christmas, but it was unrealistic. They wanted me to open gifts with them by the Christmas tree with their family. I didn't deserve it. It would be too painful. A part of me always mourned the loss of those I left behind. Not only my family but those I deserted by choice years later. Whenever I thought about moving on, I would see their smiling faces in my mind and wonder how they reacted when I left. I always hoped it was easier on them than it was on me.

28

Ashley and Craig stare at me from the other side of the booth. They are waiting for a reply. What should I tell them? They have been silent for a while, but I still can't form the words. I look again at the sheet of paper in my hands from the bottom of the stack. How could I have not seen this? After all these years of changing identities, I am still making mistakes. When I received my new social security card, I was able to change everything relating to the real Mara to fit my life events. This article I missed could lead to my demise. My heartbeat climbs.

A few years ago I remember meeting with the family who helped me falsify an ID and SSN card. I held out the cards, and they explained to whom they really belonged. I chose the identity of the woman who was no longer alive and thought it was ironic her name was so close to my likeness. Mara means bitterness, which was what I had embraced for my many years in isolation after being sick of changing identities. With each new name I gave myself, I felt more lost. How could I know who I really was? I didn't like playing the part of some hidden creature after a while. I was shaken when the messenger, and even the tormentors, knew my real name. They called me Eliza, not Mara.

Ashley breaks the silence. "I had an old friend do a

background check . . . After the accident I was upset and needed a reason not to trust you. You also seemed secretive about your past. It took a few weeks for him to get it back to me. By then I wasn't as concerned about getting it until I looked at what he found. What does this mean?"

I can't manage to say anything. My heart continues to beat fast, and my hands become clammy. I look up at the door and want to sprint in its direction.

I look at the headline of the article yet again: "Teen Gets Her Life Back After Receiving a Miracle Organ Donor." My eyes glance over the first few lines. "Cassidy Jole, a Colorado resident, receives good news after looking for a new heart to replace her failing one. There were no available heart donors in the system until the car accident occurred. The accident took the life of a young woman named Mara Lucy Woods."

I have no idea how I missed this article on the real Mara. I was so careful. I could make up a lie on the spot if I really want to. I could say I have an angry ex or family member who is trying to hunt me down. That one would work. It's a more sympathetic story rather than one with a cause for serious concern, like being a jailbreaking criminal on the loose or a fugitive. Instead, I open my mouth and nothing comes out. I could never make up a lie that huge and have them believe it. After all, the story I told them about myself was partially true. I was from England where my parents raised me. I just took out a few details amounting to around two hundred years.

"What are you hiding?" Ashley says, with more firmness.

Ashley and Craig stare at me as I sit frozen in my seat. Craig shows more concern on his face than I've ever seen before. What can I say? The truth is something they will never believe. It took decades for me to fully believe it myself. When I turned twenty, I denied the fact my cuts would heal in only a few minutes. I reassured myself some people were faster healers than others. By the time I was in my thirties, I would look in the mirror for signs of aging, but they never came. I never saw a wrinkle or gray hair but had to watch my husband get a little older each day. Ashley and Craig can never know all this.

145

"We can help you if you let us know what is going on."
Ashley tries with more care this time.

"No, you can't." I grab my belongings next to me in my
arms and gain the confidence to stand. I walk briskly to the
door and exit the restaurant. I break out into a sprint. There is
nowhere else to go but back to my apartment. I lock the door
behind me and toss my purse and jacket on the floor. I sit on
my couch, rest my head back, and let out the rush of tears I
have been wanting to release for weeks.

It was 1928 and I walked out of Ernie's Groceries with a
cloth tote bag I had sewn myself a year earlier. I looked at the
items in the bag, wondering if I needed anything more before
I returned. The family I now lived with and worked for as their
nanny let me get off earlier on Saturdays and Sundays, but this
was because I had late nights on the weekdays. I tucked all the
children into bed at the end of each evening and, exhausted
after a long day, only had a little time to read a few pages before
drifting off. I had scolded myself for not showing more
appreciation to the men and women who had helped my family
out when I lived in England. It was more work than I had ever
imagined.

This particular Saturday evening, I was able to get the
specialty food items I needed, but just as I thought I was ready
to return home, I looked up to see a bookstore open a few
shops down. I made my way past the crowds. This area of
Brooklyn had become more crowded than when I had lived
here a few years earlier. But it wasn't going to keep me from
visiting so I could grab some of my favorite missed pleasures.

Being in Brooklyn brought many memories back. I missed
the parties I would go to with Helen. I hoped she was not too
hurt by my leaving. I almost regretted leaving that identity so
early into it. But it was not a good idea to create too much fame
for myself. I wished I could have explained that to her. Back

then she knew me as Betsy, but now the family I was working for knew me as Mary. I couldn't count how many names I had been through at this point, but it was always hard when I had to shift to a new one.

I enjoyed when Helen and I would get really dressed up and I didn't have to worry as much about how much I spent. It was a shame I had to sell most of my expensive pieces of clothing. I had to embrace the shabby look suiting childcare. There was no longer any practical use for most of my clothing. I still wore my mink coat around me, not bearing to part with it. I was glad my hair had grown out long enough so I could stop wearing the itchy wig. My hair was at a comfortable length past my shoulders and dyed a deep black color.

The bookshelves in the bookstore were lit with a warm light. They reminded me of when Edmund and I would read each other our favorite lines of whatever current book we were reading. He would correct my poetry but with gentleness.

I faintly heard someone approach but was lost in thought. "Betsy?" the woman next to me said.

I turned to see Helen bundled up in her coat holding a few bags of food. I held my breath for a moment, registering my old name.

"Is that you?" Helen tried again.

I made a poor attempt to sprint away, jostling people around me. My low-heeled shoes made my feet cry out, but I continued until I was blocks away. I ducked into an alley where I waited several minutes before I was assured Helen was nowhere nearby. I almost cried. Why did I think coming back here was a good idea?

29

I am bundled up in a soft blanket watching TV, this time not eating popcorn. On the screen, I see myself going through some of the old lady clothes at the boutique. This version of me in the show I'm watching tries on different outfits and looks at herself in a full-length mirror. She can't seem to get the outfit right. I hear a quiet hissing and whispering in the background of my living room.

In my peripheral vision two shadowy figures are sitting on either side of me on the couch. The whispers and hissing get louder. I start to get nervous, but I do not dare turn to either of the shadows. Ashley's and Craig's voices beckon to me over the other sounds. "Come to us, Eliza," they say over and over. The voices are coming from beside me. I turn my head with caution to the left. The shadow looks like Ashley in a black tunic. The one on my right is Craig, dressed the same way. They scoot closer to me on the couch. "Let us help you, Eliza." They say this as their eyes begin to glow and then turn to solid black. I panic with my insides shaking but am frozen in place.

Ashley and Craig suddenly lift large machetes they've been holding, trapping me on either side. They inch closer toward me on the couch. I throw myself to my knees on the floor, then crawl pass the shadow of Craig and make my way to the window. They follow me without hurry, but the window takes a few tries to slide open. I jump out onto the fire escape and look down. It looks as if my apartment is on the hundredth floor of a building. The cars are like a line of ants below. I grasp the railing, trying to find another escape. I find the courage to look behind me. I see bodies on the floor. Where the shadowy figures once were now lie the bodies of Craig and Ashley. I jump back inside and end up stepping in their blood from their different wounds, now seeping into the carpet. I scream out and reach for Ashley's hand.

I jolt up to a sitting position and take in heavy breaths. I fell asleep on my couch without remembering, and my blanket is now wrapped around my ankles. I pull it up around my shoulders, trying to stifle the morning chill. The first of the morning sunlight is starting to peek through the small opening in the curtains and onto the floor. I take a moment to steady my breathing. That nightmare was, for some reason, more vivid than any of the others. The small relief I gained in realizing the nightmare was only a dream dissipates as I remember my conversation with Ashley and Craig yesterday at the pizza place. I grab Cosmo at my feet and embrace his furry body. He lets out a sour meow in protest.

After a few minutes in silence, I walk over to my small closet between the kitchen and the bathroom. I open it and look at the items piled on the floor, wondering when I have last used some of them. There are a few coats and sweaters on hangers and dusty boxes on the top shelf. I lift my vacuum and brooms out of the way. In the back of the closet sits a large black suitcase that has seen better days. I pull it out with much effort. I put the other items back into the closet and shut the door. I lay the suitcase onto the floor and open it. It's hard to imagine at one time everything I owned fit into it. It was only a few years ago when I moved to this apartment with nothing but a few belongings. My previous room, which I rented in a family's house, was already furnished, so I didn't have to worry about selling the furniture when I moved out. It would be much more trouble trying to sell all my apartment furniture now. I had become too comfortable. Tears threaten to fall as a bitter longing wells up within me. Never had I thought starting over again would be so painful. I had hoped for another five years in this identity before moving on.

I change into a new pair of clothes, struggling to push everything out of my mind. I leave the suitcase on the floor, not wanting to make any decision. I had treated the mundane for granted. How I wish for normal small talk with an unsuspecting stranger. Or to entertain myself with watching street performers in the park, feeding crumbs to the pigeons. I put on my coat I left lying on the floor the night before. I put some food in Cosmo's bowl and lock my apartment door behind me.

I walk briskly down the sidewalk, not sure where I am going. I have a lot to think through before I can make any big decision. It is still early in the morning, and the summer sun has yet to chase away the chill. The sun is peeking its way up, leaving golden streaks against the tops of the buildings, and long, soft shadows make their way over the street. I pass a few people jogging or walking their dogs. Maybe a quick walk will help to sort everything out. Doubtful.

I almost can't believe how much I have changed since the messenger introduced himself. Only a few months ago, I was cynical and didn't appreciate much in my life. I held on so tightly to what I had lost in the past, I felt nothing positive for my present or future. I thought I would never get any answers. I assumed I would be roaming the earth until my body decided it would start aging or until the world ended. I didn't have many answers now, but more than I had before. The messenger was the first to tell me anything that made sense. A part of me knows I can't keep running from the spirit world. It will still be there. The messenger told me that inaction is also a choice, maybe this was what he meant.

I enter the coffee shop with which I am so familiar. I remember the first conversation I had with the messenger here. I get in line as I look at the mismatched furniture and the art hanging on the walls. The barista hurries to jot down a customer's name on the cup. The familiar smell of the coffee beans surrounds me. It feels good to come back here. I do my best to enjoy everything I can about this place. Who knows if

I will be able to find another like it wherever I decide to move. The barista interrupts my thoughts. Somehow I am now at the front of the line. I have to ask him to repeat himself. After apologizing, I order my mocha and a croissant. I sink into one of the plush chairs.

Every thought of worry I tried to ignore on my walk here comes pouring into focus. I cannot sit here forever. Craig and Ashley know where I live. They will confront me again, this time not letting me leave without an explanation. How many people have they told? Enough for my identity to be in danger? They seemed more concerned for me than anything else, which is probably a good sign. Maybe nothing bad will come of it. But I just brushed them off. What a horrible friend. Why didn't I just give an excuse? Surely they would have bought one of my ideas. Then again, they probably know me well enough to spot a lie. I was never very good at being dishonest, only at twisting the truth in subtle ways.

The barista calls out my fake name. I take my mocha and croissant back to my seat. I hope this isn't one of my last moments here. I take a few gulps of my mocha. It doesn't taste right. I must have forgotten the extra sugar. My mind is elsewhere. Leaving the few bites of my croissant on the table, I go over to the coffee bar. I stir in two sugars, throw away the wooded stirring stick, and place the lid back on. I take my seat. There is someone in the chair adjacent to mine. He pulls off his hood. I almost gasp. It is the messenger once again.

"Eliza," he says. It should give me comfort hearing my birth name, but my heart feels restless.

I put my drink down on the small table between us. My hands start to tremble. How does he always know when I am here?

"There is no need to be afraid. However, there are other things you need to keep in mind."

I grab my hands together in my lap, trying to will them to stop shaking. I sit in silence. Is he here to chastise me? What could he show me that I have not already seen?

"You need to remember what it is going on around you."

151

"What do you mean?" I sputter. His words always tend to sound like riddles.

"There is a constant war going on in the spirit world. And you have forgotten."

"Forgotten? I . . ."

"The cursed spirits are looking to tear people down. Whatever they can do to discourage people . . . or distract them . . . they will do it. Even to you."

"Look," I begin, in my defense, "I was only trying to protect—"

"Your friends? Is that what you thought you were doing?" Instead of frowning, he almost looks amused.

I give him a blank look, not knowing what to say.

"I told you your heart was tested. I also said those in your life who have passed their testing have their souls protected from the Forlorn. However, this does not make them exempt from attack."

His face starts glowing, and his eyes look like they are on fire. I look straight into his eyes this time. There is a sudden shift all around me. The colors are vivid, and everything is clearer and more alive. It is as if my real life is only a piece of dust. My eyes wander around the room at the different light and dark spirits zooming about. Some dark tormentors and tempters linger around the few people in the coffee shop with the golden guardians tackling them away long enough for them to keep their tendrils away from those below. Most of the messengers are probably in the distance, giving them orders. I get a panicked feeling in my chest when I look above my head.

There are several dark spirits clinging to my head and shoulders. My head aches again. A golden spirit comes to cut them loose, but they always return to constrict me again. They must be responsible for my head hurting these last few days. I breathe heavily with panic and look over to the messenger. I gaze into his glowing eyes, and I return to the heaviness of everyday.

I put my head into my hands and start to sob. How could I have been so reckless? I thought I could get away. By running

I just gave them what they wanted. Those nightmares and the paranoia of believing everyone was watching me gave me the sense of dread they wanted me to have. They wanted me to forget the job the messenger had for me.

As if sensing my shame, he spoke to me again. "You cannot change your past choices. Instead, return to doing what is good."

"How can I know what is good?" I say with my head still hanging low.

He smiles at me. "We will be here to show you. You will be able to help many people. They will get another chance."

Every question buzzing in my mind is all coming to the forefront at once. What does this have to do with me? Why didn't I die with my family? I would have been happier than I am now. What satisfaction is there in living forever? It is a lonely existence without much meaning. Tears come to my eyes. It might have been better if I had never existed. I pick at my cuticles with my hands still in my lap.

The messenger looks in my eyes. "I know it doesn't make a lot of sense now, but it will. There is a plan and purpose for you, Eliza, even when you can't see it. All the pain and evil can be turned into something good."

I struggle to hold back tears, wiping the stray ones away. Why am I surprised he knows what I am thinking? I wish he wouldn't leave. If he stayed, maybe I could figure out exactly what to do.

"You will have a visitor tonight. Be sure to stay in your apartment this evening. I usually give you the directions, but this message needs to come directly from him."

"Who?" I ask, not having the slightest idea what he could mean.

"The Mighty One."

30

The morning sunlight is now shining through the large windows of the coffee shop. The heaviness I experienced earlier and the oncoming headache are now subsiding. I imagine the legs of the tormentors and tempters attached to my head and neck have been cut away and fewer are allowed to return now. Perhaps it took breaking down the part of me that thought I knew better and wanted to be in control. In reality, I was only running from what I knew I should have been doing all along. At the same time, I still have my doubts. I also feel the weight of uncertainty about who I would have to become and where I would have to move if I changed my name again. My mind keeps going back and forth.

I replay what the messenger said a few hours ago over and over in my mind as I eat through another pastry. I don't know whether or not I will be valuable to the messenger with all the time I have wasted. I have shown the lengths of foolishness I am willing to go in order to avoid my problems. Why would the messenger spend any more time on me if he thinks I am no longer unusable? The talk with the Mighty One sounds important, but what if it is only to say they no longer need me? They might as well find someone more capable.

I squirm in my seat, unable to get comfortable. It will be

many hours before evening comes. If the messenger really does believe everything has its purpose, why do my two hundred years seem so directionless? When my family was alive, I loved them but wish I would have listened a little more and made more out of every conversation and every minute. After they left me, I kept everyone else at a distance, also not appreciating the time I had with them. After a while I used my changes in identity as an excuse to pretend not to care about anyone. I began not to see value in myself. After all these years, what is a few more hours of waiting until evening? These little words of encouragement to myself do nothing to settle my restlessness.

Finishing my croissant, I sit back and try to distract myself with the people around me. An older man lets down his small dog, tying its leash to the back of his chair. He places his thermos on the table, then unfolds the newspaper tucked under his arm. His glasses balance on the end of his nose as he tilts his head to accommodate the angle, raising his bushy gray eyebrows upward. He gives periodic slight nods at his paper. Just like the others here, this man has no idea of the spirits all around him. A small part of me wishes for his ignorance. Living an average life seems easier. However, just because they are not aware of the spirit realm doesn't make it any less real. These people sitting next to me all have their own struggles distracting them.

I leave the coffee shop and spend a few hours walking through the park watching the people and pets pass by. It is only when I see the sun is starting to set that I head back to my apartment. The messenger said I would be giving people another chance. Am I really helping them that much? What does it mean some are lost forever? It started with the bomber in the subway. Surely someone else would have stopped him if I weren't there to do it. Many people could have died that day. What would the outcome have been for the lady on the fire escape or the man in the Chinese restaurant? The men who were in the subway at Coney Island are still out there somewhere. Levizar, their region leader, is most likely still controlling the jazz man. What was the jazz man like before his spirit was taken over? How long has Levizar had power over him?

I walk up the steps of my apartment's stairwell, still lost in thought. I lost a lot of time these past few weeks. I could have been doing something instead of ignoring the crimes around me. But what about Craig and Ashley? Doesn't their safety matter too? Yes, they were able to do a lot with their supernatural abilities. Ashley was able to save many lives through her healing. How many people would have died if she were not there? And Craig. He was the one who led us to quite a few disasters before they happened. Poor Carmen. I wish I could go back and act faster to save her. The image of Ashley sobbing over Carmen's body is branded into my memory. But I can't forget there are others who have lost a lot more and many who still will if we continue to do nothing to help. I may not see Craig or Ashley again if I decide to make a sudden move. I shut and lock my door behind me and look around, trying to find an activity to stay occupied.

I find a journal in one of my dresser drawers. It is empty, despite the many years I've owned it. Have I avoided self-reflection for so long I couldn't even pick up a pencil to write in it? I write out a few words to try to brainstorm, missing the poetry I used to write. I sit on my couch trying to jot down ideas until I come up with a few pathetic lines. I furrow my brow and wiggle my pencil back and forth. My mind struggles to focus, hopping from one subject to the next. I start to doodle in the margins.

I pause, hearing a strange noise in the background. It stops, and I continue to add leaves to the cartoon flower I have drawn. I hear it again and pause. I am somewhat fearful at this point. Cosmo is at my feet with his pupils getting larger and his fur standing up on his back. He is looking upward. I stand and glance up at the ceiling. Nothing. I sit down and continue to add a few more flowers, trying to ignore the sounds I'm hearing. The messenger said the guardians would protect me, didn't he? I hear what I now recognize as a whisper.

156

"Eliza."

I shut my journal and hug it to my chest as I stand again. I center myself in between my coffee table and the television. A slight wind blows my hair in front of my face. Moving toward the window, I am amazed to see it is shut. The wind continues. I hear the voice repeating my name. My arms speckle with goose bumps. The voice is familiar, but it is different from that of the jazz man or the messenger. It reminds me of both my mother's and father's voices, but it is neither of those either. There is something powerful, but also kind and gentle, about this voice. How could there be so much presence in one single voice?

I place my journal and pencil on the coffee table and sit down on the carpet with my legs tucked under me. Cosmo runs under the small desk beneath the window, his belly swaying with each stride. There is nothing I can do besides sit and wait for something to happen. Something moves along the bottom of the wall next to my loft bed. It crawls like a spider. I get closer and see it's a vine creeping its way upward.

The other walls have small wooden vines shooting up from every side at different speeds. There is something scratchy underneath my legs. I stand. There are small blades of grass coming up through my carpet in patches. In a few moments the carpet is almost completely covered with grass, and small flowers begin to blossom. Pink, orange, blue, and purple peonies dress the field of grass along with other flowers I have not seen before. Bushes of lavender appear, poking their heads up one by one.

My mouth is gaping, and I can't seem to shut it. Bursts of sunlight beam down from the ceiling, as if there were random skylights arranged above. The vines have almost completely covered each wall and are about to make their way onto the ceiling. They are covered in bright green leaves and periwinkle flowers blossoming in generous clumps, similar to wisteria. These flowers soon hang from the ceiling and from the tops of the walls. The walls change from the boring mandatory white to a golden color. I run my hand across the separations

157

in the wall now made up of golden bricks. They shimmer in the strong bounce light, and I can see a faint reflection of myself. My mind wanders to the day when I first noticed the change in myself. At the time, I did not think anything of it.

It was 1838, the day of my twentieth birthday, and I decided to go out for a walk with my daughter Bethany, who was now over a year old. I had asked my governess if I could borrow her to go out on a walk with me before our evening tea. I felt an extremely strange, but welcomed, energy that particular day, as if I could run a mile like it was nothing. Even in the morning, I was not groggy like usual. The sun was still shining high in the sky during our walk, and I was glad not to miss it. There were many days when I wished I could neglect my obligations and wander around for hours outdoors.

I walked with Bethany on my hip as I bounced her, looking at the wildflowers and pointing out a butterfly to her. She was beginning to say a few words, but I spoke to her as if she understood every word. She wore a white baby's gown with a small bonnet to protect her head from the sun. I only spent a few hours at the most with her each day. The governess watched her more than I did. I wanted to cherish the moments I had with Bethany. I noted to myself it would only be a few more months before Edmund and I would have to start trying again for another child.

The tree leaves in the distance looked much clearer than I had ever remembered them. I found it odd my vision seemed to improve in a day, after years of seeing far objects as blurry. I lifted the edges of my dress up so they would not snag, and made my way through the trails worn down through the field behind our property. After a few minutes of walking, I turned to go to the stables. Next to the stables, I saw the feral cat I called Buttons cleaning himself in the shade. He was the short-haired orange tabby that must have lived in the area before we did.

I reached my free hand down to him. "Come here, Buttons."

When he refused to move, I approached and reached out to pet him. He took a swipe at me and hissed. I let out a moan and pulled my hand back in disbelief. Looking down at my hand, I observed the deep cuts. I scolded Buttons, and he let out a growl before running away. When I got back to the house, I handed off Bethany to the governess and had my maid help me bandage the cuts.

A few hours later I was reading in the family's sitting room. I could no longer feel pain in my scratched hand. I peeked under the bandages and couldn't see anything. I took off the bandages and looked at my hand in confusion. Wasn't there a scratch there before? I continued to stare. I remembered feeling different that morning but in a good way. I thought the renewed energy I had felt was only from getting a sound night's sleep and nothing more. I traced the area of my hand where there should have been a scar but where there was only clear skin.

In the years following that day, I would get small cuts here and there because of my clumsiness. I tried to hide them so the others would not notice them healing in a matter of minutes. I always figured the next time I would not be as fortunate and would have to wear my scars like others. Even the few scars from my childhood were erased from my body. I learned it was not essential for me to eat or sleep, but only a habitual comfort to which I was accustomed. At that time, I was not too upset about it. It was my little secret from the world. Until my carriage accident, I had no idea how much larger of a secret it would become.

159

31

My name is whispered again. There are now small specks floating from the incredible light coming from the ceiling. I look closer and they shimmer like small pieces of gold. They cover my arms and shoulders and blanket the flowers and grass beneath me, leaving a radiant glow. I almost forget I am still in my apartment. My furniture is still present, totally immersed in the greenery. All my worries are gone from my mind, and wonder and joy fill their place.

"I . . . I'm here," I say, sounding like a child in my own ears.

"It is no mistake you are here in this place at this moment, Eliza."

"I don't understand . . ."

"I have been with you since the beginning. Not only in New York, but every time and place you have ever been. Even before you were born, I had my plan for you. I know about Edmund and your children. I also know how you have suffered wishing you didn't outlive them . . ."

I clasp my hands together as my eyes grow warm with tears. I try to push them back.

"I sent those who have prompted you along the way. You were guided, along with Ashley and Craig, to work at Sheila's Boutique so you would meet. I knew you would help each other and be more successful working together than apart."

A memory comes into my mind of a man I chatted with briefly a few years ago. He pointed out a flyer on the job board in one of the coffee shops I used to frequent. I was a dishwasher and was desperate to find a new job. The flyer said Sheila's Boutique was hiring. The man's appearance resembled that of the messenger, whom I now know him as. I can't help but wonder how Ashley and Craig heard about the job.

"There were certain things I wanted you to see before I knew you would be ready. Your years were not a waste. The condition of the human heart is growing worse on Earth. People refuse to give up what they think is theirs. They think they have control, but by hardening their hearts to pride, they end up losing everything."

I nod, remembering what the messenger said about those who are taken over by the cursed spirits. I wait to hear what the voice will say.

"It is far worse than you know. The tormentors and tempters know they will eventually go to the Forlorn and want to take as many with them as they can. When people harden their hearts, these cursed spirits attach themselves. When people have spirits attached to them and then they pass on, they are brought to the Forlorn. They become whom we call the inconsolables, because by then they have run out of chances. You are sending the cursed spirits to the Forlorn before they can get what they want."

"The messenger told me about the Forlorn . . . but what is it exactly?"

On the wall next to my bed, the vines separate, opening to a blank space on the brick wall. After a few seconds a small black swirl starts to form in the middle of the blank area. It resembles a small vortex and increases in size with each moment. Pretty soon, the darkness covers a few feet of the wall, now moving more slowly. It resembles a screen looking into a distant place.

I make out the horizon in the darkness lined with jagged, leafless trees reaching their boney fingers upward in every

161

direction. They reach up to a starless night sky, which has no light except for an odd moon having a deep red color. Its redness illuminates the top of a small farmhouse which looks worn and abandoned. The house sits on a flat field strewn with sharp rocks and tumbleweeds blowing by. I hear faint screams in the distance, but the words are too indistinct to make out. I see what appear to be dark tendrils that are revealed only faintly in the red moonlight. The creatures with the tendrils enter the farmhouse through the broken windows, and the broken screen door slams behind one of them. The rocking chair on the porch lets out a creak behind them. A few crows line the roof seemingly observing all the commotion.

The visual brings me through the door of the house. The sobbing is getting louder as my vantage point goes further into the house. A faint silhouette sitting on the kitchen floor in the corner comes into view. As I am brought closer, I see it is a woman. She is wearing a dress made of scraps, and her tangled hair pours down over her face. The woman is hugging her knees and rocking back and forth. What I see now are cursed spirits circled above her making hissing noises. Her cries become more desperate. One tormentor makes a shrill laughing noise in between the hisses. Its tendrils wrap around her body. As she screams, one of them wraps her throat, so she starts to choke. The image on the screen fades, slowly turning to a solid black. The screen dissolves, and the brick wall appears empty as it did before. I rub my arms, noticing a tingling sensation making its way up my spine. I shudder, feeling horrible for the lady. The Forlorn is way worse than I could have imagined. This is why the messenger is so insistent on me continuing to fight the dark forces. The inconsolables who are trapped not only are lost but will be trapped in this place filled with torture and devastation. Would I have continued fighting for people if I had known what I know now about the Forlorn?

"This is why your task is so important. Many harden their hearts and do not see the consequences until it is too late. They refuse to let go of their pride. When you send the tormentors or tempters away from a person, you enable them to choose a softened heart. It gives them another opportunity. A heart I examine that I find has replaced pride with humility and turned from its need for control to repentance, I will forever keep safe. Only I can fully see the state of a person's heart."

"What about mine?" I was told I was tested but haven't been able to remember.

"Your heart was searched when you were young."

Another vortex is forming on the wall. This time it is more golden in color. It gets larger until it is as big as it was before. The screen fills with an image of two beds in a room with a warm glow lit by the sun. There is a small girl on her knees, sitting on the end of one of the beds. She looks to be around the age of four. As the details become more apparent, I recognize the doll she is hugging as my own from childhood.

A few minutes earlier before this scene, I remember I had snuck into the kitchen to steal some of the pastries our cook had just made. My mother had found out, scolded me, and sent me to my room. I had felt guilty even before I was caught. I cried a lot of tears, wanting to tell her I was sorry. I was upset at myself for doing something I knew I shouldn't have. I would always lie by blaming my sisters or our pet dog, but now I wanted to turn away from my dishonesty. Again and again I reached out in my mind, begging to say I was sorry and wanted to change. Was there someone listening who had a bigger plan for me and the other people in my life? I wanted to be told it would be all right; I hoped someone like me could be forgiven.

The four-year-old version of myself stops crying and looks around the room. She begins to hug her doll tighter. The wooden vines begin creeping up the sides of the room again. In only a few minutes, the room is transformed to look how my apartment does now. She hops off the bed as it is almost submerged in vines, along with the other furniture. "Eliza," I hear the whisper in the screen say, as if in response to the request of my four-year-old heart's plea. It was soft but powerful, carrying an importance and weight. The voice knew my name. It heard my cries and answered.

163

I hear my younger self squeak out a reply. "Yes?"

"I have searched your heart and know it. I am here when you think you are alone. Because you have transformed your heart to one of repentance and cried out to me, your heart will be safe. You will have many difficulties in your life, but remember, in the end it is not the evil that wins."

The girl, the young version of me, has no response. A flower appears in the room. It twirls and floats downward. She sets down her doll and holds out her hands as if knowing she should catch it. The flower is a rose with many petals and is the size of her head. She lets it land in her hands, observing it more closely. It is gold and glistens in the sunlight, yet it is light in her small hands.

"This is my gift to you, so your heart will be protected even until the very end," the voice says.

My younger image studies the rose. Her eyes get big as the rose starts to dissolve. It melts away, petal by petal, but rather than falling away, it runs into her skin. Its glow creeps up her arms and down her body until she is completely saturated with it. Her face looks radiant. She falls to her knees in awe of what has just happened to her.

"You will live many years. You will stop aging at twenty years old. For many of those years you will wander and curse your own life. Throughout those many years, you will witness the human condition and its depravity. Humans naturally turn away and choose what is not good for them. The cycle continues. One day I will want you to give others the same opportunity you have had. I will give you the strength you need to stand against the evil torturing those people. I will be with you always."

The screen fades out again until there is only the golden brick wall in its place. How had I not remembered this moment at all? Maybe I had mistaken it for a dream at some point early in my life. Or maybe I chose to forget it.

"Why . . ." I am not able to voice my question fully.

"What you see as a curse of not aging, Eliza, was really a way for you to see how the world is darkening. It is only getting worse. You have viewed in person generations desperate for an answer to their misery. They are searching but for all the wrong things. Your human body would also be too fragile to enter the spirit world without this strength I have given you."

Only a piece of me grasps what he is saying. It should have been someone else. Someone better. I am the most unlikely choice of all. I am small, unintimidating, and unnoticeable in a crowd. But I'm also pessimistic. Nothing is ever good enough compared to what I had. I should have appreciated Edmund and my children more when they were alive. I have allowed myself to drown in my own grief and have become a miserable person. I let the bitterness eat away at my heart. When I am shown a challenge, I find any way I can to escape it instead of confronting it. I would rather stay comfortable than take chances.

"You are valuable, Eliza. You see yourself as small and weak, but I am the one who gives you strength. If you thought you were strong on your own, you wouldn't see a need for us. You have the chance to continue using the abilities I have given you so others will be free."

As the Mighty One says this, a burden is lifting. He knows what I am thinking and what he is saying is true. New seeds of hope begin to be planted in me. Instead of focusing on who I should have helped, I want to focus on what is left to be done. I watch the golden flakes as they continue to pile up on my shoulders, and my regrets melt away. Maybe the two hundred years were worth it after all.

A gust of wind blows in my direction, forcing me to hold my breath. It stops, and I look down at a yellow piece of paper on the ground. It has creases from being folded and unfolded. It sits under a beam of light coming from the ceiling as if under a spotlight. I pick it up. The wind must have blown it out of my jacket pocket. I forgot I had left it in there. I smooth it out, looking at the cartoon of the sun playing a saxophone. My heart palpitates a little when I see the dates at the bottom. This music festival is only a week away. I had never told Craig whether or not I was willing to help him stop the events in his dream from happening.

"The festival is another chance for you to confront Levizar and the spirits under his control. Once you send Levizar to the Forlorn, the cursed spirits will be weaker and less able to have influence over his region. I have given Craig his dreams and Ashley her ability to heal when their hearts were examined years ago. You were all prompted in order to meet with each other at this time. The evil done will be replaced with something good. You can be sure you and your friends will join me one day when all the evil has been destroyed. You will see your family again and also Carmen."

I will actually get to see my family again? Does he mean at the end of time, or will I cease to live forever and start aging? I let out a breath of relief. Carmen is not totally lost. We will see her again one day and be able to explain how we were able to take down those who took her life. There is a new hope— rather, a hope I had not understood before. If our bodies are destroyed, we will be safe even then.

Is it safe for me to face Levizar, or the jazz man, again? How many more people will we have to free from the tormentors and tempters before it will be possible to overcome him? I want to ask if I can be given a number to know for sure, but I look around and notice the vines as well as the flowers are starting to recede. They fold up, as if growing in reverse, not withering or fading. Pretty soon my apartment looks the way it did several minutes ago. I do a double take, trying to figure out how it all happened so fast. Was this a dream? But I was awake the whole time. No, it felt more real than anything else. I go to my bathroom mirror and see the golden flakes on my hair and shoulders. My face is glowing and nearly too bright to look at. I hear one last whisper in the distance.

"Don't be afraid, and remember the hope you have. I will always be with you."

32

Stirring my coffee, my spoon makes a clinking against the sides of the mug. I watch the swirls of coffee turn from a dark black to a creamy brown color. Creamer and sugar have always been a must for me ever since I started drinking coffee in my early years in New York. I decided it would be better to have coffee at home this morning instead of going out. I wrap my blanket around my shoulders, still wearing my flannel pajamas and fuzzy socks. As I stare out at the city from my single window, I take small sips of my coffee. I fold my legs under me and prop my elbows on the edge of my small desk beneath the window. The golden sunlight shines on the top halves of the buildings as the traffic noises begin to increase below.

I take in deep breaths. The warmth of the coffee moves through my body as I take small sips. Last night, I decided to eat ramen in front of a Chillflix show. I slept more soundly last night than I had in weeks. No nightmares disturbed me. The painful headache that would come and go everyday disappeared. I no longer felt the anxious worrying creeping up inside me.

Despite having many things to be concerned about, I feel a strange and unfamiliar peace. Somehow I was not scheduled for this weekend but am scheduled for an early Monday morning shift tomorrow. I can't just not show up. I need this job for now so I can save up.

I pick up my phone and click on my group text with Ashley and Craig. My thumb hovers over the screen's keyboard for a moment. I scroll through our different texts relating to different memories together. A bittersweet smile forms on my lips. What will I say? There is no running away now, especially after all I know and all they know too. We still need each other. The music festival is on Saturday, less than a week away, and I can't do it alone. How can I make this work?

I throw on some clothes and pat down my hair before pouring myself another cup of coffee. I continue to stare down at my phone on my desk, as if this will help the words come to life somehow. I jump, hearing a knock on my door. I look through my peephole and open the door. Craig and Ashley look to be in good spirits despite the way I brushed them off the other day.

"Can we come in?" Ashley asks in a cautious way.

"Uh, sure." I prop the door open and step aside.

I close the door behind them and motion my hand over to the couch. As they sit down, I ask them if they want anything to drink. It is more of a formality than anything to ask, but they say they are fine. Ashley has her hands buried in the pockets of her hoodie, and Craig has his hands clasped together with his thumbs fidgeting. We take brief glances at each other, while otherwise our eyes scan the room with no real focus.

"We wanted to check on you and make sure you were doing okay," Ashley begins.

I nod. "I'm sorry if I was dishonest before. I just don't know how to explain it in a way that would make sense . . . or not have you think I'm crazy."

"It's okay, you don't need to—" Craig starts.

"But I do need to. I need to tell you a lot of things. First of all, both of you are really special to me. In these past few years I haven't had anyone I could honestly call friends. Not even close. Many times I wouldn't even try to make meaningful connections. Quite the opposite actually. I would go out of my

168

way to be distant with anyone near me in my life. I thought it would make things easier. I had lost too many relationships. I thought if I just stayed away, everything would be fine again. I could finally put my pain away and start over on my own."

I have their attention, but I can see they are unsure if they still want the truth yet curious enough to keep me going. Don't I owe it to them?

"I soon discovered this was not the case. I remember you invited me out to pizza even though you hardly knew me. Ashley healed my neck without worrying about what I would think of her. Both of you made sure I had someone to talk to. All you wanted to do was help but I kept resisting. I'm sorry if I pushed you away."

I can see tears starting to pool in Ashley's eyes. She dabs the corners of her eyes without smearing her makeup. Craig cleans the smudges off his glasses with the corner of his shirt, wearing a serious expression.

"We also wanted to talk about something that happened last night," Ashley starts.

"Really? What was it?" I look over at Ashley.

"Craig and I were texting about visiting you this morning . . . when he mentioned someone visiting him last night . . . and I also had someone come to me."

"Who was it?"

"He called himself the Mighty One. Does that sound familiar?"

I smile and nod. "Yeah, he visited me yesterday too."

"I thought I was going insane at first," Ashley goes on, "but then Craig said he saw similar things."

"Well, you are a little insane," Craig teases her.

Ashley gives his arm a little shove and rolls her eyes.

"Anyway . . . Do you remember what you said about the heart testing?" Craig asks me.

"Yeah, what about it?"

"I was shown when mine happened. I can't believe I hadn't remembered it."

"Me too," Ashley interjects.

169

"Did he also show you what the Forlorn is and mention the festival?" I look at both of them.

They give me a nod. "It looks like an awful place," Ashley begins, "and with the festival only a few days away . . ."

"I know. I see now why it's so important to take action. I thought I was doing the right thing by keeping you guys from all the bad stuff happening. I thought ignoring it was the best way. No matter what, there will always be something awful going on, at least for now." I say these things knowing I am explaining it rather than justifying it like I had done before.

"It will be okay. We will figure it out." Craig puts his hand on my shoulder for a moment, trying to comfort me.

"There is something else you need to see," I tell them.

I take in a big, controlled breath and then walk over to my dresser next to my bed. I open the bottom drawer and put a few items aside. I approach them with a few framed photos with items balancing on top, which I place on the table in front of the couch.

Ashley and Craig scoot apart so I can sit between them. I pull out one of the larger framed photos from the pile. I run my fingers along the edge of the bronze frame trying to remember the last time I went through these. It probably wasn't since I had moved to this apartment. I study our faces in the photo. It was taken a few months before my daughters Scarlet and Violet became sick.

In the photo my family is positioned in what we called the sitting parlor, wearing serious expressions and looking into the camera. I am sitting in the middle in a cushioned chair, with the larger lower portion of my dress covering my legs and feet entirely. My sleeves are long and puffy with the top of my dress covering my collar bone. I have my hair pinned up. Edmund is behind me, wearing a large mustache. He is on the left, with his one hand resting on the back of my chair. His other hand is behind Lily who is eleven in the photo. Bethany, the oldest, is on the other side of my chair with her hand on Martha next to her. The twins, Scarlet and Violet, are sitting on the ground trying to keep Andrew still, who is on the ground in between

170

them. Andrew looks a bit blurrier than everyone else, not able to keep completely still.

"I told you I was originally from England . . . and I actually was."

"This is . . . your family?" Craig asks.

"Yeah, this is them," I say as I pass the photo to Ashley on my left. I smile to myself, knowing Craig probably assumed the people in the picture were dead relatives I never had the chance to meet.

I take out another photo from the stack. This one was taken many years later; it's clearer but still in black and white. In the photo, I am wearing a short bob with my dirty-blonde hair. My head is slightly tilted upward, and I am giving a sideways glance into the camera with my tweezed eyebrows arching upward in a sassy expression. I'm holding up a cigarette in one hand while my other hand is tucked under the opposite arm; my fur-trimmed coat rests around my arms below my bare shoulders. I'm wearing a satin dress with a string of pearls hanging from my neck. How the times had changed between the two images of myself. I hand the photo to Craig and bring out a few other headshots from my life in the twenties.

"These were also a part of my life."

"Are these also of a family member?" Craig asks.

"Not exactly." Now I am wondering if it was a good idea to show them.

"Wow, she looks pretty. Like an old movie star or something." Ashley studies another headshot.

I pick up an old corset I had kept. It is tattered and now more brown in color than the off-white it used to be. I study the lacing in the back and the whale bone giving it its structure. I remember how many times I would curse it for making it hard to breathe when doing anything more than a slow walk.

"This is my corset. It was in much better condition a while ago. Now it looks pretty old."

I hand it over to Ashley, then pick up my old brush. The carvings on the back of the ivory are very detailed, much more than anything modern-made. Edmund smiled when I opened it and saw it for the first time. Most of the time, I insisted on brushing my own hair before Louise would pin in up for me. There were still strands tucked into its bristles.

"This was a gift from my husband for my thirty-fourth birthday." I hand it to Craig.

"Your thirty-fourth birthday? You are married?" Craig wears a bewildered look.

"It was a while ago. He passed away quite a few years ago now."

Ashley and Craig look back and forth between the photos and my old items from England. They don't seem to understand yet. What would I say to them? It all seems ridiculous.

"These are pieces of my life. My very long life. I know you probably won't believe me. At least I will know I am no longer lying to you."

"What . . . How . . ." Ashley fumbles over her words, looking back and forth several times at me and my portrait in her hands.

"That photo was taken when I lived in Brooklyn. After all the years of changing my appearance, I could never manage to leave New York for very long before coming back."

"Look, Ashley. She has the same beauty marks on her neck." He points at the photo Ashley is holding.

"The Mighty One must have been telling us the truth about her old age. But how can that be?" Ashley says. I wonder what other things they were told last night.

"This is her somehow, but . . ." Craig turns to me and asks, "How old are you really?"

"Do you really want to know?" I give him a smile.

My friends have been here for me all along. A heaviness in me starts to become light. They would not reveal my secret to others, after all. Before, they might have had reasons to believe I was hiding ulterior motives. Now, it is up to them to trust what they have experienced and what the messenger and Mighty One have said. We were all guided here for a reason, and our abilities won't go to waste. It will take a while for Craig and Ashley to believe my true age, but they are trying. No matter what happens at the festival, we will all be together using what was given to us to do something good.

The year was 1905 and I decided I was no longer satisfied with traveling as a lifestyle. For three years I had traveled to many different areas around Europe without buying a home of my own. I would go from one hotel to the next. At first it was thrilling to see new places because I could pretend I was on a trip where I would soon go back home to Edmund and my children. Only in the back of my mind did I admit the reality of my situation. My home had been another person's property for a few years now. I would never see Edmund and my children again.

When I was in my house, I realized I could not live in it any longer with all the walls, floors, and furniture saturated with memories, but it would be foolish to waste all my money without plans of settling down in a home. The large sum of money I had made from selling my estate was trickling away more quickly than I wanted to admit. I could not squander the provisions I had left or I would end up on the street. I obtained a passport with another new name and bought a ticket to ride the steamboat to Ellis Island in Manhattan.

I held onto the railing of the ship with my gloved hands. The sea and sky met in a layer of fog, as if the sea was holding up the sky. The boards of the ship creaked under my feet as I struggled to fight the nausea that came with the gentle rocking of the boat. Even after a week at sea, I could not overcome my seasickness. A few others stood beside me. One of them was a woman holding her son. Her husband was in New York waiting for her. I cabined next to her and joined her for mealtimes and entertainment above deck. I was grateful not to sleep underdeck like most aboard. The foul stench of urine and body odor from below was enough to make anyone vomit.

A few more people joined us on deck. We looked toward our destination together. It was as if we could sense it approaching. The passengers were headed to America for different reasons. Some had family members go ahead of them and were to be reunited in a new country. Others were traveling back to their home country. And then there were those looking for new opportunities. Rather than being intimidated by this new journey, I chose to view it as a chance to start over. I could be whoever I wanted to be in America. I had enough money left to rent a small place and not have to rush to find a profession, so I was ready to make the most of it.

A contagious murmur broke out among the people as we came closer. A few minutes later, the speck broke out of the fog and we could see Lady Liberty. I felt a new hope and joy. What would my new life look like? The others around me also appeared to be asking themselves this question. Someone clapped and a cheer rang out in the air as we joined in the applause. My face became sore from smiling. Soon we would be on land and I could begin my new journey.

33

I knock on Ashley's door, carrying a fabric tote bag tucked under my arm. It contains my purse and a few items of clothing she told me to bring with me. I wait for several minutes, debating with myself if I should knock again. It is several hours before the start of the festival; even the sun has not yet shown itself. I made sure to ask Ashley if she was going to have coffee at her place. She agreed to provide coffee and donuts for us.

Today is Saturday, the day we have been anticipating, albeit nervously. A few days ago over dinner, we studied the map on the back of the flyer showing the streets blocked off for the festival. Fifth Avenue would be blocked off from Madison Square Park to Washington Square Park. The other diners would have never guessed the anxiety we were feeling. The potential outcome of this event was more than enough to make us uneasy. We continued to joke around like usual, but I could tell it was just as heavy on Ashley's and Craig's hearts as on mine. Not knowing what the jazz man was planning limited us in how much we could prepare. Craig only gave us a vague idea of what would happen from what he saw in his dreams but nothing certain.

Since the day I showed them my old pictures and keepsakes, I still couldn't tell if they believed me yet. At least they were trying to make me think they did. Maybe a part of them wants to trust that it's true, and this is enough for me. After I told them my real name and facts about my family members, they began asking strange questions of minor importance. When we were at work, Craig asked me how people went to the bathroom in Victorian times if there was no plumbing. I explained how, before bathrooms existed, people had to use either the outhouse or chamber pots in their bedrooms. He laughed when I said standing up to use the chamber pots was made easier for women because their undergarments were, for many years, crotchless. I am relieved I no longer have to keep the secret of my age from them.

I knock again.

"Be right there!" Ashley yells.

"No worries," I say once she opens the door. I barely recognize her in the outfit she's wearing. It's a black short-sleeved turtleneck tucked into a dark plaid skirt up to her waist. Ashley's brown hair is tucked under a black-hair bob wig with bangs, with a black beret sitting on top of it. A beaded necklace hangs around her neck. I close the door behind me and see Craig is already here. He gives a wave, and I return with a smile.

"What do you think? Did I do a good job or what?" Ashley holds out her arms and shakes her hips. I purse my lips, managing to contain my laughter.

"Um . . . it looks great. Very beatnik." I pour myself a cup of coffee from the carafe on the counter.

"Isn't it a little much, though? I thought we were trying to stay hidden?" Craig asks.

"Well, hidden but working in style." Ashley picks up a pair of sunglasses from the table and balances them on the tip of her nose. She puts one hand to her hip and wiggles her eyebrows at us.

I break out into laughter. "I can't say I would recognize you if I saw you on the street."

"Don't worry. The outfits I have planned for you guys are not as over-the-top as mine. I just have to go all out, you know?" Ashley and Craig join me at the table for coffee and donuts.

We have discussed the idea of disguising ourselves, figuring it will be harder to help people in the future if our names are revealed to the public. Ashley got super into it. Her enthusiasm for the fashion challenge could not be extinguished. The other day when we were looking at the map together, she took out her sketchbook to ask a million questions regarding what our disguises would be. Ashley talked aloud to herself about wanting to grab the essence of the festival and put it into our outfits. We needed to embrace the cultural and artistic history of Greenwich Village, of course. As she sketched away, she asked me what was worn in the beatnik days. I gave her a few examples. When she asked me what my personal life was like during that time, I blushed and said I didn't really want to get into it. I convinced her those days of my life were really not worth talking about.

I finish the last gulp of my coffee and wait for them to finish as well. We discuss when we need to leave and where we will start looking for the crimes to happen. We talk in a more serious way than we have in the last few days, knowing it is almost time. Going over the timeline with each other may help but is also a reminder we don't really know what we are doing. Anything could happen. I try to enjoy my time with Ashley and Craig, unsure what we will face and clinging to the hope I received from the Mighty One.

Ashley hands me a wig, and I grab my bag and head to the bathroom to change. In a few minutes, I come out wearing the black striped shirt I bought from a secondhand clothing store, tucked into my high-waisted black jeans. My wig is also a jet-black color with bangs tickling my eyelashes. Unlike Ashley's, mine has long, scraggly hair that hangs to my waist.

"Wow, you look amazing!" Ashley squeals. She puts a beaded necklace around my neck, and I pull the back of my wig hair over it. She turns to Craig. "Your turn!"

Craig lets out a sigh and slumps his shoulders as he takes his bag with him into the bathroom. I sit with Ashley waiting for him to come out.

"Your outfit looks great." She untangles a part of my wig. "Thanks for going along with it. I know both of you aren't into fashion as much. It's just the first time I have thought about putting something together since . . ."

"It's no problem really. The outfits are great." I give her a smile and squeeze her hand.

Craig steps out of the bathroom. "I guess it's not that bad." He, too, is wearing a striped shirt but his is underneath a long-sleeved denim shirt rolled up past his elbows. His ensemble includes dark blue jeans. His face drops when he sees Ashley come at him with a wig and a short beard to cover his clean-shaven face.

After a few minutes of prodding from Ashley, Craig dons his short, curly wig and matching beard.

"Uh, this is pretty uncomfortable already, Ashley." I can tell he is already tired of the whole façade, and we haven't even gotten started. Compared to ours, his costume makes him look the most different, although he still wears his usual thick-framed black glasses. He looks scruffy and sloppy, opposite of his usual NYU-student look.

"Stop scratching it!" Ashley slaps away Craig's hand from his wig.

I start laughing at him through my nose when I see the look of disdain he gives Ashley.

"What's so funny?" Craig shifts his gaze to me.

"Nothing, I was just remembering something funny in the movie I watched last night," I reply. Ashley and I grab our sunglasses and head toward the door. I tuck my phone in my pocket but decide to leave the rest of my belongings at Ashley's place.

We walk down Fifth Avenue as the sun is starting to greet us. There are only a few people walking the streets at this hour, and those we see are setting up their tables. The festival does not start for another few hours. I wonder if it was a mistake coming so early. But the jazz man and his men will most likely be here before the start of the event. It would be much better to catch them before the festival is flooded with people, before

178

any real damage is inflicted. I rock back and forth on my heels as we stop to look around.

One of the stages is going through a sound check. A woman with pink hair is speaking into the mic while a man nearby adjusts the audio board and another double-checks the equipment. A few rental vans are parked on the outskirts probably holding more audio equipment. According to the map, there will be another stage in the middle of the street and a third one at the other end of the block. Some of the tables being set up are pretty small, like the face painting and craft tables for the kids, while others are much bigger. The larger ones belong to businesses ranging from real estate to jewelry.

As we make our way down the street, we see a hot dog vendor in his truck and another man setting up his popcorn machine. I see a cotton candy machine and remember how determined Carmen was to get some the day we went to Coney Island. I don't think she ever ate any that day. My heart flutters. Hundreds of people will come here from all over the city, country, and beyond to celebrate. Pretty soon the street will be filled with these festivalgoers. One woman with a clipboard and earpiece is going around making sure the barricades are placed properly. I don't see anything yet to cause alarm.

I see two men on the security team talking to each other over cups of coffee. I'm relieved they are here, but also notice they don't have guns on them. The screams and the groans of the subway victims rush to the forefront of my mind. I see the great force behind the machetes and the crumbling of bodies all around me. I try to swallow, and my saliva catches in my throat. How many more times would we have to witness terrors like these, Craig's nightmares becoming reality? I close my eyes and try to control my breathing. Craig asks me if I am okay, and I give him a nod. He gives my shoulder a squeeze. I can see the tenderness in the way he looks at me. How I hope we all make it out okay.

179

34

A few hours have passed, and we are now in the middle of all the festivities. The pink-haired lady finishes singing her song with her band, and the audience explodes in clapping and cheers. The next artist comes up on stage and introduces himself. He has prepared a slam poetry piece. He tells us to promise to look him up when we get home. His pleading is saturated with desperation and his performance, below average. I can't help but cringe. A girl next to us is holding her dad's hand and skipping down the street. She is holding a balloon animal, and her face has been painted with a glittery mask. I can smell the greasy yet tempting smell of hot dogs and kebabs in the distance. The scent of buttery popcorn also reaches my nose. More children walk with their parents holding painted artwork and wearing pipe-cleaner necklaces.

I insist we get some food. We step with caution so we don't stub anyone's heels or get mowed over by a stroller. Shoulders are bumped and a few apologies are shared before we finally reach the food area. We buy hot dogs from the stands and balance our food and condiments in our hands while searching for a place to sit. I place my food on one of the tables and grab two more wooden folding chairs for Craig and Ashley.

Another girl with a painted face passes by Ashley. "Wow,

the face painting designs are really cool!" Ashley stares into the crowd as if looking for more designs. "Do you think I'm too old to get one?"

"No, I think they'd give you one," I tell her.

I take a bite of my hot dog and lean back in my chair. The sun feels good, not too hot despite our layers of costume. I lick the ketchup from the corners of my mouth after devouring my hot dog, then wipe my mouth with a napkin. I lean back into my chair again and close my eyes. This could be such a relaxing day. The Mighty One told us we needed to be here, but I'm hoping it ends up being less dramatic than the way Craig described it to us in his dreams. I wish everything could stay peaceful like it is now, but that's only wishful thinking. I remember how fast the trip to Coney Island turned into chaos. We were resting on the beach one minute, and the next, people in the subway were scrambling for the exits.

As I open my eyes, I see a man in a dark gray jumpsuit and black cap exit onto one of the side streets near the barriers. He lights a cigarette and leans up against the wall of the building. The man takes drags of his cigarette as he talks to himself. I see an earpiece wedged in his ear. I excuse myself from the table and make my way to the side of the building so he does not see me.

"Yeah, there's a lot of people today . . . Yeah, totally . . . We should start in a few minutes . . ."

What does he mean, "start in a few minutes"? Did he mean the performances?

"Okay, sounds good . . . Bye."

What am I supposed to think? What would he say if I confront him? If he sees me, would he run? Would it hurt to check?

The man's steps are coming toward the edge of the building in my direction. My feet are frozen to the pavement. I recite the first phrase the messenger gave me. A light floating sensation comes over me with a crisp clarity in my vision. The man is now in front of me. The dark spirit above him is tightly fastened around his neck. I shudder as it gives an unworldly

181

cackle. Its tendrils pulse. I remember the headaches and horrible nightmares. It would be only a small piece of what the man is going through.

"In the name of the Mighty One, you will leave this place and enter the Forlorn." My voice holds a new confidence as it bounces around the objects in the spirit world. I now have a knowledge of what the phrases mean. The souls of the found could be forever kept safe. This man should get the same chance. The tormentors and tempters must have their power taken from them so they are unable to destroy anyone else.

I sink and return to the fogginess of the physical world. The man is looking around as if stunned. He does a double take when he sees the black bandanna around his arm. He unties it and lets it fall to the sidewalk. The man notices me and takes off in a sloppy sprint away from the festival. I pick up the bandanna to look at it. My hands tighten around it with an inkling of fear spreading through me.

Tired already, I return to my seat next to Ashley and Craig. If I feel tired after one tormentor, how will I deal with several of them and the jazz man? I lean back in the chair where I ate my hot dog only a few minutes earlier as I hand Ashley the bandanna.

"What is this?" Ashley asks me, not knowing why I would be handing it to her.

"I faced a guy in a dark gray jumpsuit over there." I point in the direction where I was standing. "It looked like he worked here . . . but something felt off. I went into the spirit world, and I could see a tormentor was attached to him."

Ashley's eyes become wide. "Where did he go?" Ashley looks around, her eyes dodging over the crowd of people.

"I'm not sure. He ran away but not until after I was able to make the tormentor leave him. He threw the bandanna on the ground before leaving."

"The Notorious gang . . . Do you think the rest of them are here?" Craig asks us.

"Maybe. I'm not sure." I tell him. In my mind I see the men wearing black flashing past me in the subway. The bandanna

182

Ashley is holding is identical to the ones those men were wearing.

We sit for a moment of silence, viewing the crowd and hearing the music and chatter in the background. I am confident he would not have come on his own. There is at least one other I remember seeing in the subway. We must be vigilant. We have spent the first few hours of the festival enjoying it more than searching for them. Hopefully the others are dressed in a similar way so we can spot them without much difficulty. What direction did he come from? Was anyone else with him?

"I'm starting to feel drained already. What if . . ." I start voicing my vulnerabilities.

"We believe you can do it," Craig says from across the small table. "And if you need anything, that's why we are here. Let us know what we can do."

I nod, not exactly sure what to tell them I will need. I hope I can ask for help when the time comes.

It was nearing the end of 1868, only a few weeks after my false death. I took careful steps along the slick cobblestones still glistening from yesterday's rain. I thought about what Edmund had told me of my funeral. Some of the lesser acquaintances had said I was a dear friend. I was a strong mother and a faithful wife. I had a cheerful disposition. I laughed to myself. What did they think about me when I was alive?

The sky was blanketed with gray, and almost everything was damp and dreary. With the sun hidden, the warm-colored limestones of the buildings now felt dull and worn. The dark street lamps stood in rows with their flames flickering and swaying. On either side of the street, shops with tall glass windows displayed their items of specialty, ranging from clocks, shoes, and jewelry to different cuts of meat.

I stopped to study various shops as people in the street passed by. I was wearing a black dress and a bonnet with an attached veil drawn over my face. Edmund and I told others that I, as his great-niece, had a husband who had passed away. My fake husband had left me with very little, and I had no one to provide for me. This story gave me at least two years before I had to explain my attire. I imagined if I wanted to go to town in the following years, I could simply invent another family member's death in order to wear my mourning clothes again.

I peered into each window, grateful to be able to get out of our house. I was not sure how solitary of a life I would be living, but I was more afraid that I would be recognized. I kept my head low as people walked by me. An older man and woman looked at my face. My heart fluttered but then calmed as they continued walking. They looked like the type of people who might have been guests in our home, but I couldn't place them. Three businessmen on the other side of the street were discussing a business proposition. I was not sure if I would look at a crowd of people the same way again. I could not help but examine anyone who passed me. I was waiting, with panic and dread, for someone to spot me and call out my real name. I would be facing only doom if they did.

35

A half hour has passed since we finished our meal, and we have paced up and down Fifth Avenue without sitting to rest. We've checked every booth but have seen no one resembling the man in the alley. We watched a few songs from a band playing at the Washington Square Park end, then headed back toward Fourteenth Street soon after. The tops of our cheeks are red from the sun. Ashley plops down into one of the wooden folding chairs. We end up sitting where we were eating before.

I straighten in my chair when I hear a crashing sound. Have I imagined it? I hear a scream followed by more cries of panic. People a few feet down the road are scrambling around each other. It's the same survival desperation of the subway. One of the rental vans in the distance, its driver out of view, is swerving back and forth down the street catching as many bodies as it can. The crowd is packed so tightly, the men, women, and children struggle to get out of its path. Some get out of the way only seconds from being crushed. Others are not so fortunate and are caught under the tread of the tires. One woman screams as she rolls up onto the hood of the van and then slumps to one side. The uproar of the screams becomes more intense as the van approaches.

"Come on!" Craig yells at us to get up.

Adrenaline races through my body. Ashley and I follow Craig as he hurries to the sidewalk. The moment I turn around, the chair I was sitting in is toppled and crushed under the weight of the vehicle.

I stumble over my words. "Open my eyes and allow me to see the truth behind the inner movements of every life." In a panic I manage to get the words out and find myself light, yet the clarity of this world makes the weight of evil feel enormous.

The tormentor is wrapped around the driver's head and arms as if his tendrils are the strings to his puppet. More people try to get away from the van, falling under the tires.

"In the name of the Mighty One, you will leave this place and enter the Forlorn," I scream out my second phrase before the van is out of sight. The tormentor and the others near it shriek and explode into tiny splinters dissolving into the air. A loud crash rings through the air and reverberates off the buildings as I am brought back down to my body.

The van's hood is steaming, having smashed against a building. Popcorn litters the street, and the popcorn machine is now on its side. My body feels very heavy. I did not fully recover from the last tormentor I faced. With each cursed spirit I take down, I'm only adding onto my exhaustion. Ashley and Craig stand beside me as I sit on the curb with my head in my hands. I would lie down on the sidewalk if it were not so dirty. The man in the van gets out and looks around as if he doesn't know where he is. Two security guards chase him down the street until they tackle and handcuff him.

"Um . . . I'm going to . . ." Ashley points to the injured people.

"Yeah, go ahead. We'll catch up with you," Craig replies, and Ashley runs off to try to heal those who were hit first. Hopefully she will reach them in time.

I let out a deep sigh.

"Are you okay?" Craig sits next to me.

"It took a lot out of me that time." I smile, trying to reassure him I am only tired.

In a few minutes the joy and excitement of the festival have

186

turned into mass confusion and terror. A woman next to us sobs with her hand over her mouth, trying to comfort her daughter on the ground whose legs have been crushed. The girl's father is on the phone calling for help, doing his best to hold himself together. There are chair and table pieces all around us, and debris from the craft and jewelry tables litter the street. Several bodies lie in awkward positions in smears of blood. Many cries of adults and children are heard in the distance. All other onlookers appear dumbfounded and in shock.

From the other end of the festival come more screams followed by additional crashing noises. I get a lurching feeling in my stomach. I stand up and struggle not to vomit. It is too far down for me to see anything clearly. A loud explosion and rapid popping sounds pierce my ears. I cling to Craig's shoulder and hold my stomach as I force myself to take steps in the direction of the chaos.

"I-I can't do it." I look up into Craig's eyes. "I need to get over there." His eyes search mine.

Without warning, Craig scoops me up with one arm under my legs and one under my back. I let out a faint gasp. He takes long strides toward the commotion. I am like a small, feeble child in his arms. We go much faster than if I had dragged myself on foot. I try to focus on what my next move will be once we get closer and not the fact that I want more than anything to curl up in a little ball and fall asleep in Craig's arms. I do my best to keep my drooping eyelids open.

I revisit the horrible nightmares. The cockroaches crawling up my skin. The shadows of Craig and Ashley staring at me. My missing face in the mirror. Yanking at the doorknob while the jazz man approaches me from behind. I recall the panic of being watched, looking around in a constant paranoia, and the intense headaches I couldn't explain.

And then there are the emotions I cannot run away from. The self-doubt and self-loathing. Am I enough? After all these years, can I turn my failures into something good? Were all these years a waste? Am I too far gone? How can I press on knowing I would leave those I loved behind? Will I ever see my family again? If I moved on in love, would Edmund understand? Could I live with the guilt if I decided to move on? The weight of all the questions is unbearable.

The messenger told me I had a purpose and a plan that was made just for me. Any evil done in this life can be turned into something good. The tormentors and tempters were not impenetrable. The meetings with the Mighty One and visions of his testing of my heart as a child come to my mind. The visions of those who ended up in the Forlorn were frightening. It was what we have been trying to prevent. Then there were the gentle reminders. The powerful and reassuring voice. *Don't be afraid, and remember the hope you have. I will always be with you.*

We get closer to Washington Square Park, and the noises get louder. Craig stops and sets me down on my feet. There is another large rental vehicle driven into the side of a building. The popping noises continue, this time much more terrifying. My heart begins palpitating, and my palms become sweaty. My breathing quickens. The man on stage is wearing a tattered peacoat and fedora. The fedora shadows his eyes. His fingerless gloves grip an automatic gun. He throws it back and forth in a wild sort of way, scattering what is left of the crowd. A deep laugh comes from parted lips. Goose bumps speckle my skin. My hands jump up to my neck, as if the bruises he gave me were still there. The ghost of pain is still there. I struggle to repress my memory of it.

Craig and I hide behind one of the few booths left standing near the sidewalk. I turn my focus from the armed gunman on stage to the motionless bodies on the street. Will Ashley be able to help them in time? There are more people down on this end than the other. One man jumps out in front of his two children but ends up being taken down by the jazz man. His son and daughter run from out of shooting range but let out shrieks as they turn around and see their father on the ground. One young man cries out for his wife who also did not make it away fast enough. She reaches out an arm toward him, but her injuries do not allow her to get up.

"Eliza." My breath catches as the jazz man says my name. "I know you are there. You cannot hide forever." Each sentence from the jazz man feels like it lingers in the air with a hiss.

I cling to the Mighty One's encouraging words, letting them overwhelm the other voices trying to convince me to give up and run away. I teeter. I hope my will to continue will sustain my weakened body. Craig's hands grab my shoulders to keep me from losing my balance. Unable to reply, I lay my hand on his in gratitude.

I whisper, "Open my eyes and allow me to see the truth behind the inner movements of every life."

I become light and drift upward. I view the spirit world once again. Dark and light spirits are colliding into one another in an intense ongoing battle. The smoke of the dark spirits seems nearly to cover the street in a blanket of darkness. The spirit hovering around the jazz man is the darkest of them all. This tormentor, Levizar, holds every part of the jazz man's body with a constricting grip.

As Levizar rises in the air, he grows rapidly in size, now five times what he was before. He turns into a hideous monster as he grows, resembling a creature with sets of moth-like wings and legs like those of a black widow. His three heads have several eyes on each one and pincers out front click together. Even in the spirit world, my skin crawls. Levizar makes hissing and clicking noises before speaking.

"It's no use, Eliza. You are destined to fail. You are nothing." He follows with a laugh.

I try to continue. "In the name . . ."

The jazz man, enraged, sends several shots in my direction. I cringe as I can feel the ache in my body below. I don't know how many times he was able to get me, but the pain is undeniable. I become heavy but try my best to fight it. If I slip back into my body, it will all be over. I won't have the energy to try again. I can tell Craig is holding onto my arms, gripping tightly so I don't fall over. I tell myself it will be over in a few minutes. Everything will be fine soon. I have to keep trying. I must press on.

"They don't care about you, Eliza."

"In the name . . . of the Mighty One . . ."

"They are just using you."

"You will leave this place . . ." My voice cracks as I struggle to get the words out.

"Once they are done with you, you won't matter."

"And enter the Forlorn!" I say at last in a soft voice.

A loud and ugly scream erupts from the mouth of the terrifying creature. His legs crumble underneath him and start to wither. His wings droop. With a loud clash, he splits into thousands of moths swirling around until they dissolve and are gone from sight.

As I grow heavy and return to my body, the jazz man now looks like an old, confused musician who doesn't know what is going on. With extreme care, the jazz man places the gun down on the stage. He falls to his knees, crying. I feel severe pain in my legs and stomach. A large blood stain is soaking through the stripes of my shirt. The full impact of my pain sweeps over me. I collapse, and Craig catches me before I hit the ground. He props up my head on his legs while my body lies on the pavement.

The jazz man is still on the stage. For a moment his upturned face is glowing. The glowing of his face is similar to the vision of my younger self when my heart was being examined. This man will probably have to spend many years in prison, but he will no longer be a prisoner of the darkness that entrapped him. In this way he will be freer than he has ever been. It could have just as easily happened to anyone else.

Craig begins to say something, but I don't understand his words. I struggle to keep my eyes open as Ashley appears in the distance. She is placing her hands on more of the injured, and as they sit up, healed, their family members and friends react with exuberant relief and thankfulness. My body will begin to heal itself soon, but I cannot escape the exhaustion. I drift off.

36

I struggle to blink away the blurriness. Something is tickling my eyelashes. I reach to push it back. Something itchy is on my head. I brush back the scraggly hair from the wig. Why am I wearing this? What has happened? I prop myself up with my arms. A strange-looking man is sitting next to me with a wild beard and curly hair.

"Hey." Craig's voice comes from beneath the ugly beard.

"Where's Ashley?" I don't see her.

"I think she saw where we went. I'll text her just in case." He pulls out his phone.

I grimace. My shirt and pants are soaked in what I believe is my own blood, but I am no longer bleeding. I feel a pulsing ache from the bullets inside me. The jazz man shot me. It all makes sense again. I am probably more tired from scaring away the tormentors and tempters than from the bullet wounds, but those don't help me either. Craig's legs are also bloody and still bleeding.

"Are you okay?" I ask him. He has asked me this more times than I can count.

"I think only one bullet hit me, and the others just cut past me."

"Hopefully Ashley will get here soon."

We are on a side street away from the festival and away from anyone. Craig must have carried me here. I can't seem to remember that part. There are only hushed tones coming from the blocked-off street. A loud joyful event turned into a screaming and sobbing spectacle in only a few minutes time and then has concluded in near silence.

Craig and I sit in silence. Distant sirens wail in the background. A few minutes later a silhouette approaches. Ashley runs in a crooked line, trying not to trip over her own feet. When she reaches us, she bends over with her hands on her knees, attempting to catch her breath.

"Wow, I am out of shape!" Ashley breathes heavily and bends down next to me.

"Don't worry about me. Heal him first." I motion toward Craig.

Ashley places her hands on Craig's legs and hands him the bullets. I can see his eyes bulge in amazement, even behind his glasses. She moves in my direction next.

"Dang girl! That's amazing! Can you do it again?" Craig asks her while she is in the middle of healing the wounds on my stomach.

"Not unless you want to be shot again . . . Don't think you want me to shoot you!" She gives him a sideways glance and a wry smile.

"Well, I wouldn't take myself out of harm's way exactly," Craig jokes.

Ashley motions toward the bullet wounds on my legs. "I will be healed in a few hours anyway," I explain.

"Yeah, but you probably are still in pain. Why not do it right away?" Ashley says, and I nod in agreement.

Ashley cuts open my jeans with Craig's pocketknife to get to my leg injuries. Her hands are warm and tingly against my skin. She hands me the bullets, and I thank her. She sits in between us. The denim from my jeans is flowing at the sides of my cleaned-up legs. I could not have imagined what would take place at the festival, but I'm glad the three of us have survived. Ashley sits in between us and hugs her legs with her

192

head down. Her smile fades, and she looks toward the ground.

"What's wrong?" I prod.

"I really tried, I did." Ashley buries her head in her arms.

"What do you mean?" I ask her.

"I wasn't able to save everyone . . . If only I had been faster."

I put a hand on her shoulder as she starts to sob. Craig gives me a concerned look. Craig and I wait for her to say something more. I want to ask her how many people she could not help. I also want to point out how many people she was able to save, but I refrain from doing so because I can sense she is not ready to hear it. Ashley has done everything she could, but to her it may never feel good enough.

It was a cool autumn day in 1837 and I had just given birth to my daughter Bethany a few days prior. Bethany was the first of my children, and motherhood was all new to me. My body was still aching, and the labor process took a few more hours than I had expected. The pain was also more than I imagined. It would probably be the same way with my recovery. As I lay in bed with her beside me, I remember thinking, "It was all worth it." Her tiny eyes stared back at mine. She seemed so small and fragile.

I let Bethany grab my finger with her little fist. Her arm had popped out of the blanket she was swaddled in. In my room the curtains were drawn, and I had many weeks of being in bed, which began toward the end of my pregnancy as a period of confinement and rest. It would continue for a few more days until I could venture around my home and then outside. I would finally see guests again and spend more time with Edmund. Although it was tedious to stay hidden in the dark, away from the rest of the family, I was glad not to be wearing my pregnancy corset and also to be given the chance to recover without the responsibility of my daily tasks.

I was glad the pregnancy and birth were over. The world would still be a dangerous place for Bethany due to the high mortality rate of infants at that time, but I was grateful to have made it this far. So many other women could not say the same. There were many who lost their babies before birth or even their own lives in the process. It was not uncommon then. So I felt eternally grateful. I almost could not believe my body had created such a beautiful treasure, nor had I understood the love I would feel for her after she was born. I wanted to guard her with all that I had. I held Bethany close to me and promised I would do anything I could to protect her and help her grow up to be happy and safe.

37

I sway back and forth with my arms tightly crossed. Ashley and Craig are standing beside me. The coffee line is longer than usual for this time in the evening. I am antsy as the line has barely moved since we arrived. In the past few days, we have heard many news stories about the festival and ongoing investigations about who the men were behind the attacks. We left the scene before anyone could interview us and our identities were hidden with our disguises so they couldn't track us down later. Someone might have mentioned something about Ashley's healing and raised suspicion. The reports show several discrepancies. The men come from different cultural and socioeconomic backgrounds. No one can figure out a clear motive. All three men ended up getting arrested. I remember seeing a clip of the jazz man where he looked collected although solemn.

Our workday at the boutique was pretty typical, except we joked around way less than normal. It was pretty silent in the store, just a handful of customers all day. Craig and I agreed we would spend more time with Ashley. No matter what she says, she still needs our support. Ashley stands next to us with her hands in her pockets. Her silence is unsettling, similar to the way she was after the subway attack.

We get to the front of the line. Craig offers to buy our drinks and says we can get whatever we want. He knows Ashley and I struggle more with our finances than he does. He would rather pay for our drinks or meals than to have us not come. After we order, we find a free square table and pull up a third chair from someone else's table while we wait for our drinks. Ashley is propping up her head with one hand while her other one is scrolling through something on her phone. She is wearing an absent expression. Craig gives me a look as if to say, "Should we say something?" I shrug.

Craig's name is called and he collects our drinks; he struggles to carry all three at once. Ashley ordered an iced coffee and Craig, a white mocha. I would normally make fun of him for ordering a "girly drink," but not today. I leave my mocha the way it is, not feeling up to adding any sugar. I take sips of my mocha, contemplating what I should say to Ashley. I don't want to regret my words or my silence.

"I couldn't do it." Ashley is gazing downward, with one hand around her drink resting on the table.

"What do you mean? You helped a lot of people," I point out.

"But I couldn't get to them all. There were a few who didn't make it."

"There would have been a lot more who didn't make it if you weren't there."

"So what?!" Ashley snaps at me.

I look at her, unsure of what to say. Would Ashley begin to avoid us in her anger in a similar way she did after Carmen's accident? I'm hoping she doesn't cut us off. I want her to know we are here for her, but I'm afraid I'll something that will cause her to isolate herself again. Will continuing to tell her she did the best she could help her or drive her away?

"Sorry . . . it's just . . . one of the girls I tried to help was around Carmen's age." Her voice catches. "No matter how much I try to get back to normal, I just picture Carmen asking me why I didn't save her. Every time I can't help someone, it's a reminder. I see Carmen's body . . . so mangled . . . It's just not fair." Ashley begins sobbing into her crossed arms on the table.

I put a hand on her shoulder, and Craig does the same. I try to hold back my own tears watching Ashley in her pain. Memories of Carmen come to the forefront of my mind. I remember the way she would bounce in her seat at the pizza place and take huge bites out of her pizza. I smile as I envision Carmen playing with her dolls in the corner of the boutique and how she tried to convince us her doll needed jewelry. My hand still knows Carmen's little grasp while waiting for Craig and Ashley to be done with their roller coaster ride. I swallow back my tears as I remember Carmen's pink bunny sitting on the platform of the subway and the sounds of Ashley sobbing over her body.

38

The sky is turning a deeper shade of blue. The sun is slipping below the horizon sooner than I expected. I zip up my jacket and slip my hands into my pockets as the breeze gets colder. I stand with Ashley, Craig, and a small group of neighbors at Washington Square Park. Cars are driving along Fifth Avenue as if nothing ever happened. Only a week ago last Saturday, it was littered with debris and the dead bodies of those who could not escape fast enough. What was supposed to be a joyful festival ended with overturned booths and broken tables and chairs. The inventory that was sold from the tables looked like trash dumped on the street. The street is now clear, looking like it had before the festival.

Ashley's face is glazed over, not looking at anything in particular, and she has dark circles around her eyes. She holds a medium-sized bin with her arms cradling it. We were instructed to bring extra candles just in case. Ashley wouldn't let anyone else carry them.

"You sure you don't want me to hold it?" Craig asks, for a third time.

"No, I'm fine, really." Ashley gives him a faint smile.

My gaze drifts over to several people gathered under the giant arch. They are displaying photographs of loved ones as well as flowers. Any minute now we will be told to light our candles. Would the victims still be alive if Ashley had been quicker? This is the question still haunting Ashley. Knowing she did all she could do is not enough for her. What can I tell her to make her feel better? A word-packaged cliché or a greeting card line does little to help comfort anyone. Ashley cannot see that if it was not for her, over a hundred more people would be dead. There were only three who died before she could help them.

A few days ago the messenger found me again at the coffee shop. He praised us for helping defeat Levizar, but I wanted more answers. I had to ask him what happened to those three who did not survive. He gave me a knowing smile.

"I knew you would be concerned, Eliza," the messenger explained. "You see, when you recited the words I'd given you to Levizar, you also expelled the other cursed spirits around him. The three people who died—two women and a girl—were among those. They were able to have their hearts examined and passed before they slipped away. This will not always be the case. There are many who are killed in violence before they choose the right decision."

One of the pictures in the center of the park vigil is of a little girl. A lump rises in my throat. At work earlier that week I told Ashley what the messenger had said about the three having their hearts pass their testing. It gave her some relief, but I expected it to help her more than it did. If it lessened her burden, she didn't let it show. In her mind, what she did was still a failure. I remember Ashley's face when she first saw Carmen's body on the train tracks. I couldn't make myself look for very long. The image would never leave her. She would have taken Carmen's place if she could have, even the place of the little girl in the photo. Craig and I try often to remind her how important she is to us. I have a feeling she will need more reminders.

A woman shouts above the background chatter of the attendees and tells us to come toward the center. The candle lighting will begin in a few minutes. I join Craig at the center near the arch. Ashley has finally put the bin at our feet and slipped away from the crowd. I tell Craig I'll be back in a minute. She is at the hot cocoa station, which is set up on a large white folding table and manned by volunteers. I stand beside her as she tears open a powder packet and dumps it into her cup of hot water. I hand her a stirring straw.

"Oh, thanks." She looks up, finally noticing me there.

"No problem." I give her a side hug, squeezing her shoulder.

After stirring in the powder, she takes a sip to test the temperature. She still appears distracted.

"I had a daughter once named Scarlet." I continue when she doesn't stop me. "She always had so much energy, not even the governess knew what to do with her. In fact, the governess almost quit. I would get upset at Scarlet for her carelessness. A broken vase here. Another rip in her dress . . . I couldn't ever be mad at her long, though. She always had the funniest remarks . . . I would look down at her and tell her what she did was not acceptable. She would look up at me with her large eyes and say something like 'That's okay, Mum, I can always glue it back together.' My anger would soon melt away. I admired her ability to persevere."

Ashley stands with both hands holding her cup of hot cocoa close.

"There was a point where she didn't make it through. She was only seven. So young. What appeared at first to be a small cold turned into something bigger in a few short weeks. She looked so helpless and small in her bed. Her energy and spark were fading a bit more each day. I had to sit there and watch it happen. She was slipping away and there was nothing I could do. I would have given anything for her to get better . . . After she . . . it was a long time before I could accept it. I still don't know if I have. It's like there is a small part of her still with me. A small piece of each of my family members is still with me."

Ashley wipes a tear away from the corner of her eye. I wrap my arms around her, holding the embrace for a while before pulling away.

"People say it gets better. That you will move on. Even if it's true and they mean well, it doesn't help. I may not have the right words, but I know you were the best sister for Carmen. And I know you miss her."

"Thank you." I put my arm over Ashley shoulder, and she wipes away a few escaping tears as we make our way over to Craig. We stand on either side of him.

"Is she all right?" he whispers in my direction.

"She will be . . . eventually." I smile up at him.

The lady in charge of the event tells us in a loud voice that a few volunteers will be coming around to light a few of our candles. Once our candle has been lit, we can light the candle of the person next to us and so on. An older man comes to give us the paper rings for our candlesticks so the wax won't melt onto our hands. He then lights my candlestick a moment later. I hold the candle out, afraid my hair will catch on fire. I pass my flame to Craig's wick, and he lights Ashley's candle next to him. Some men and women are setting down their larger candles in the center near the framed photos and bouquets.

I hold my candle with one hand, watching a bit of melting wax creep down the side. Craig next to me interlaces his fingers around mine and gives my hand a squeeze. My hand is comfortable in his despite mine being so much smaller. I blush, surprised but in the best way possible. I have wished for his attention for a few months now but have not let myself act on it.

"When I was very young, my parents insisted I get married. They only gave me a few months." I look up at him.

"How old were you?" Craig asks.

"I was only seventeen when they told me. Only a few months later I was married to a man I had just met."

"Wow, that is young."

"My dad was sick and wanted to make sure his daughters would have a secure future. I wanted so badly to speak up and say I wouldn't do it. That I wanted to take my time finding someone. I wanted to make sure I knew him well and wait until

I was older."

"I'm guessing you didn't?"

"No, I couldn't say it. I ended up marrying Edmund. I thought my life was over. I didn't think I would ever be happy, at first. I would have to live with a stranger and manage his home, knowing very little about responsibility to begin with. I was forced to grow up very quickly."

"How did it work out?"

"It was rocky at first. I got to know him a little more before we got married. We were constantly learning new things about each other. I had to take on a lot. In a few years we built our family, and it seemed silly we'd once thought of each other as strangers."

"That does sound like a lot."

"Before I knew it, the years had passed by and I was sitting beside the bed of an old man."

I wait for him to pull his hand away from mine, but he doesn't. He watches me, waiting for me to continue.

"Even in his old age I stayed by his side. I watched him pass and eventually each one of my children as well. Throughout the years, I've had to let go of a lot of people I loved. I always knew I would be noticed if I stayed around somewhere more than a few years. It's mandatory I change my identity no more than every ten years." I look around, making sure no one is listening.

His face begins to look serious.

"I can understand why you wouldn't have believed me when I told you I lived that long."

"The Mighty One told us you outlived your family and you grew up before the turn of the century. I thought it sounded impossible. Even crazy, in fact. But from everything we have seen and experienced, I know I can trust what he says. Don't blame me if it takes a while to get used to the idea."

"What? Hanging out with an older woman?" I tease him.

Craig smiles back at me, and I can tell he is searching for a comeback but can't find one.

"I'm sick of changing identities. It's a lot harder than you would think being disconnected from people. Very lonely most of the time. The other day in the pizza place, I was about ready to take all my stuff and leave."

"But you didn't."

"I couldn't do it."

"I'm glad you didn't. I don't want you to leave. Ever."

Craig squeezes my hand again. Heat rises to my cheeks as I look down at my boots.

"I had an interesting dream the other night."

"Oh, really?" I ask.

"Yeah. It wasn't one of those scary dreams either. You were in it."

"Me? What was it about?" I am surprised he also has good dreams about the future.

"It wouldn't be any fun if I told you, would it? I'll be sure to tell you one day."

I feign disappointment with a pouting face and tell him it's not fair he won't tell me. He laughs and puts his hand around my waist. I lean into him. I realize the guilt I've felt in the past is gone. I used to think Edmund would be disappointed with me if I ever fell for anyone else. But this feels right. Edmund would understand. Craig is more than just a crush. He has proven to be a great friend with the potential to be more. We make a great team in our ability to help people together.

The flame from my candle bobs up and down in the breeze. My candle is now dripping on all sides, but the paper stops it from burning my hands. The sky is now engulfed in total darkness. What future tasks does the messenger have planned for me? He will probably approach me within the next few days or weeks. No major crimes will plague Manhattan for now. I will have to move on to another location to find the next region leader. I need to focus on being in this moment. The warmth of Craig's arm around me. The cold biting at my nose. A community coming together. I absorb it all around me as my eyes scan the crowd. The flames dance, blanketing the night as one as their tiny flickers bring light to the darkness.

Acknowledgements

I would like to thank my editor Deb Hall for all the work she did on this novel! She has taught me a lot and went above and beyond. She was also really patient with all of my questions!

I would also like to thank some of my beta readers: Ruth White, Jen Honeycutt, Jen Coss, Mila Sacarelos, and Emily Pemble. I appreciate getting feedback on how to improve my story.

I received much needed information on what it is like to live in New York. Thanks to Carissa Basuini for the inside scoop on being a local who could give me tips on how to add some authenticity.

I also appreciate the time that my mom and husband took to read through my story several times. Thanks for the advice on how to make this story better!

I want to recognize the font author Peter Wiegel for the two fonts used on the cover.

Find Out More

To find more information on upcoming projects and books, check out the websites listed below!

facebook.com/elizahartseries
artofcandaceball.weebly.com
instagram.com/candaceballart